ROYALLY ENRAGED

HER ROYAL HAREM, BOOK FOUR

CATHERINE BANKS

TURBO KITTEN

Turbo Kitten Industries™

P.O. Box 5012

Galt, CA 95632

www.turbokitten.us

Catherine Banks

www.catherinebanks.com

www.turbokitten.us/catherine-banks

CHAPTER 1

JOLIE

"**S**top trying so hard and just do it," Leona said with a shake of her head. "It's like fighting. You don't focus on what move to make next, you just block the kick and punch the guy in his stomach."

"Yeah, once I know how to do it," I argued, but focused and tried again.

Fox sat on a patch of grass in front of our house, growing pieces of vines and braiding them in a long rope. I attempted to change his attitude, to make him angry, but he just kept smiling and braiding.

I sank to my knees on the grass with a sigh. "I'm pooped. I can't do anymore."

Leona patted my shoulder and sat beside me. "Your stamina is improving at least."

"My stamina of not being able to do anything? Wonderful." I hung my head.

"Lunch!" Rhys called from inside the house.

Fox turned and smiled at me. "Done for today?"

I nodded.

He picked me up under the armpits until I was standing, and then kissed me. "Good, because I have something fun planned for us."

"Okay." I returned his smile despite still feeling a bit defeated. We hadn't seen any trace of Justina or Brayden, aka Triton Douche, in four months, and while I was glad to have time free of danger, it worried me. I was certain they were planning something and I wanted to get stronger, so I could be an asset in their defeat.

"Make sure you eat protein," Leona ordered me as she followed us into the house. "And a bit of sugar."

"Yes, ma'am," I said and saluted her.

"I'm going out," she said and headed for the garage behind the house. "I'll be back tonight."

"Oh, are you on your way to visit a werewolf with a special hammer?" I teased.

She smiled, undaunted by my teasing. "You know it! I'm still trying to convince him to use that hammer on me."

Fox burst into laughter.

"Have fun!" I called to her as we walked inside.

"What's so funny?" Deryn asked Fox.

He shook his head. "I am not repeating that."

"What's for lunch?" I asked, kissing Deryn on the cheek before following him down the hallway.

"Not sure. Nico made it," he said with a shrug.

"Nico cooked?" Fox's eyes widened and then he ran down the hallway, disappearing from our view.

Nico was a great cook, so I totally understood Fox's desire to get there and start eating.

Deryn linked our hands and squeezed. "You okay?"

I looked up into his handsome face. His dark eyes were focused, the corners pinched in concern.

"I'm fine. Just tired from using so much magic. Also, frustrated because I still didn't accomplish anything," I said and frowned.

He squeezed my hand again. "You're improving. Leona told me you are."

"Not fast enough," I whispered.

We made it to the dining room, and found Rhys, Fox, and Nico sitting at the table. The table had several main dishes and side dishes.

"What's this?" I asked. "What's the occasion?"

Nico stood with a wide smile, his eyes sparkling with warmth. "No occasion. I just felt like cooking you a delicious meal."

I walked to him and gave him a deep kiss. "It looks and smells delicious."

He pulled out a chair for me and pushed it in when I sat.

We chatted about random things while I stuffed my face. Once finished, I relaxed back in my seat with a satisfied sigh. I gazed at Nico "That was amazing."

"I'm glad you enjoyed it." He kissed my cheek and began cleaning up.

"Let me clean," I said and tried to push him out of the way.

He smirked. "How about we clean together?"

I nodded and took my place at the dish washer. He scrubbed, I put the dishes in, and when they were done, we would both put them away. It was a system we'd worked out recently.

"Come on," Fox said. "It's time for our date."

"Date?" I asked.

He nodded. "Remember? I said I had something fun planned for us."

"Right!" I agreed, smiling wide. I kissed Nico and then followed Fox out of the house. "Where are we going?" I asked.

"It's a surprise," he said. "You'll see when we get there."

We went into the garage, a huge building with room for eight vehicles. Currently, there were four, one for each of my mates. I had asked about getting my own car several times, but they preferred that I ride with one of them. Plus, Thor often drove us around anyway.

Fox's car was a sleek, silver sports car. I had no idea what the make or model was, just that it was pretty and *super* expensive.

He opened the door for me, and I climbed in.

"Ready?" he asked as he started the vehicle.

I nodded and buckled up.

Our fun date ended up being a trip to a karting place. The guys were planning on building one at our house, but kept arguing over details, so it wasn't finished yet.

Fox paid for us, completely ignoring the looks the women at the counter were giving him. I brushed my thumb over the mating crystal beneath his eye, and he kissed my palm. "I love you," he whispered with a wide smile.

My heartbeat became erratic and I returned his smile. "I love you too, Foxfire. So much."

His smile turned cocky. "I know."

I laughed and smacked his chest lightly. "Butt."

"I do have a nice one," he said and glanced over his shoulder. "Though, I notice you looking at Deryn's more."

I rolled my eyes. "Yes, you have a great ass. And, I do look at yours a lot. I just do it when you aren't looking." I winked. "I can't let your ego get too big."

We walked to the track, and I realized that no one else was there. The entire place was empty.

"Did you buy out the entire track?" I asked him. Not that it would surprise me. My mates were stupidly rich.

He nodded. "Yep."

Not a single ounce of remorse. That was my Fox.

He helped me put on a helmet, and then we climbed into a couple karts.

A teenage-looking male walked towards me and said, "Head over to the start line. There will be a horn signaling you to start.

You get ten laps. I'll wave a flag for the final lap and then the finish flag. Got it?"

I nodded and saluted him. "Yes, sir."

He rolled his eyes and stepped back so I could go.

There was just a gas and brake pedal, plus the steering wheel of course. I could drive a manual transmission, but I was glad that the kart was so simple. I lined up in the middle of the starting line and Fox pulled up on my left.

"I'm going to destroy you," he said with a wide smile.

I opened my mouth to reply, but Deryn replied before I could. "Not a chance! This time, you'll eat my dust!"

I turned and stared in shock at my other three mates, all in karts lined up beside me.

"You guys!" I yelled.

They chuckled.

"I wanted to surprise you," Fox said. "I originally planned for it to be just you and me, but it's just so much more fun when it's all of us."

"Tonight, you and I can have some alone time, since you sacrificed our date," I told him.

"Now, I'm jealous," Rhys said.

He wasn't. My mates were never jealous of each other. Something that my brain had a hard time understanding. Just the thought of them with another woman made me see red.

"Easy," Fox said and reached over to rest his hand on my forearm.

I exhaled and shook my head. "Sorry."

"We're yours," he whispered. "You don't have to worry about that."

I smiled at him. He always seemed to know what I was thinking. "I know. Sometimes just imagining it is enough to make me mad."

"Well, stop imagining it," he said and laughed.

I kissed the back of his hand and then put the visor on my

helmet down. "Prepare to lose!" I threatened all of my mates. I turned to Nico. "No magic."

He pouted. "I wasn't planning to, but fine. I'll play fair."

"Only if he is winning." Rhys chuckled, and Nico flipped him off.

"Ready?" the bored teenager asked while chewing on some gum.

"Ready!" we all yelled.

I gripped my steering wheel, a huge smile splitting my face.

The horn sounded, and I slammed my foot down on the gas. The kart was much faster than I thought, and I squealed in delight as it shot forward. I bumped into Deryn, shooting him a wide smile as I continued on. The first turn came up, and I didn't slow down. I waited until I was right at the turn to slam on my brakes and jerk the steering wheel to the side, making the kart drift around the corner.

"What!" Fox demanded as they chased after me.

I laughed loudly, but it was cut off as Rhys caught up to me. I swerved in front of him, preventing him from passing me.

"Hey!" he yelled.

"Cheater!" Deryn yelled.

"It's called winning!" I yelled back.

"We've been played!" Nico yelled. "She's raced here before!"

"No one asked!" I reminded them, drifting around the next turn.

I had come here twice before I moved to Jinla. I'd been trying to figure out where to live and what apartments to apply for at the time.

Deryn and Fox were on either side of me as I drifted, and I couldn't help the joyous laugh that escaped my lips.

"It's on!" Fox yelled.

"Already thought it was," I teased, letting my words float over my shoulder as I took the hairpin turns before us.

Nico shot past me, and I gasped. "Cheater!"

He winked as he held the steering wheel in one hand, flexing his free arm's bicep. "Nope. Just pure skill, baby."

"Isn't that my line?" Rhys asked, slamming into Nico's side and making both of their bodies shudder from the impact.

I heard the teenager who worked there sigh, but didn't look for him. I knew we weren't supposed to hit each other, but I also knew if we broke the karts, we would pay for replacements.

I charged after Nico and Rhys with Fox and Deryn on either side of me.

The teenager waved the final lap flag, and I was too busy laughing at my mates' shenanigans to care that I came in last. I clutched at my stomach as I continued to laugh.

"Again!" Fox yelled as I pulled past the finish line.

"This time I won't go easy on you," I teased, driving my kart back to the starting line.

He said something in another language and we all lined our cars up. Nico winked at me and I saw his fingertips glow slightly. What was he up to?

The horn sounded and we all took off. All of us except Fox, who was stuck at the starting line.

"Nico!" Fox yelled.

Nico laughed, and I high-fived him as I drove beside him.

Fox's kart was finally freed from Nico's magic and he raced after us.

Each race had different results, but each was just as fun as the last. After the tenth race, I parked the kart to get some water and take a break. The guys continued racing, and I took a seat on the viewing deck to watch them.

"They're so gorgeous," one of the girls said. She had long blonde hair that brushed her hips and startling blue eyes.

"I bet they're amazing in bed," the other girl with tanned skin and brunette hair said.

The girls looked to be in their early twenties, but I wasn't sure. They were both beautiful, but neither had a bloodstone. They caught me looking and just stared back.

"They are amazing in bed," I said. "Mind blowing."

Their mouths dropped open.

"You're their mate?" the blonde asked.

I nodded.

"Wait! You're the Siren Princess!" the brunette shouted.

I nodded again.

They took seats at my table.

"What's it like?" the brunette asked, her eyes wide and cheeks slightly reddened.

"What?" I asked.

"Being with four males?" she clarified.

"At times, frustrating. Think about your relationships and how you have to take into consideration their feelings and wants. Now, multiply that by four," I said.

The brunette cringed.

"But, I love them and they love me. They're a lot of fun, as you can see," I motioned at them laughing and racing each other still. "They're the most caring males I've ever met and do all they can for their people."

"Can you make people fall in love with you?" the blonde asked. "Is that how you snagged them?"

Anger boiled within me, but I quickly shoved it down and shook my head. "No, we can't make people fall in love with us. If that were true, I would have had a mate long before I met these four."

"And that would have been a pity," Nico said from the chair he now sat in beside me.

The girls yelped and jerked back in shock at his sudden appearance.

"What's up?" I asked, turning to face him with a smile.

He kissed my cheek and then trailed a finger down my jawline. "Just wanted to touch you."

That was something we'd both been doing a lot lately. I smiled and kissed his lips lightly before looking at the other three, still engaged in an intense race. "Thanks, for coming."

He stood and kissed my forehead. "Anything for you, my flower."

He disappeared and was in his kart in the next instant.

"Whoa," the brunette whispered.

"You get used to the teleporting," I said with a smirk.

"No, you weren't kidding about them loving you. He really does love you," she said, her eyes slightly unfocused.

"What are you?" I asked.

She blushed. "Human, but I can see auras. When he was with you, his aura was pink, full of love. I rarely see that, even with couples who have been together for decades."

"Survive a few life and death situations together, and your bond runs pretty deep," I told her. My smile didn't waver despite the bit of pain that flared in my center. So many painful memories. Especially, the one of me trying to kill Nico.

All four karts slowed and I shoved the memories away, letting the joy fill me again. "Want to hear some stories no one else has?" I asked the girls.

The karts resumed their intense speed.

I told the girls a few funny stories, ones I knew the guys wouldn't care about being shared, and then walked down to the track. All four were removing their helmets and putting them away.

"Dinner?" I asked them.

"Dad invited us over," Deryn said.

I smiled. "Great! I haven't seen Dan this week."

"I know. He keeps reminding me," Deryn muttered. "'It's been four days since I saw her. It's been five days, Deryn. Deryn, where's my daughter,'" Deryn said, mimicking his father.

My mates' parents loved me, all except Nico's father, Johann, anyway. It had taken quite awhile for Rhys's mother, Adelaide, to accept me, but I had finally gained her approval.

"I know you've been wanting to see the twins, too," Rhys said.

Rhys was talking about my ex-boyfriend Martin's twin daughters. I was their unbiological aunt, and I tried to see them at least once a month. But, the last two times I had visited the werewolf den, they hadn't been there.

"Are they there?" I asked.

Deryn nodded. "Yep, Dad confirmed that they are there tonight."

My smile widened. "Great! Let's go."

I climbed into Fox's car and let him drive me, since it had been his idea for us to go on the date. He held my hand as we drove, and I relaxed in the passenger seat. Fox was a great driver, calm and attentive.

He parked at the werewolf den, and we waited for the rest of the guys to arrive before we headed to the house. Dan opened the door and pulled me into a giant hug.

"Hello, father," I whispered against his incredibly wide chest.

"Daughter, you've been gone too long. You need to visit me more often," he chastised.

"I'm sorry. I've just been busy with my lessons," I explained.

"I told him," Leona said from inside the house. I couldn't see her because Dan's massive body was filling the entire doorframe.

"How did I know you would be here? You heard free food and couldn't stop yourself, could you?" I teased her.

"You never look a gift horse in the mouth," she reminded me.

Dan stepped aside and let me enter the house.

When I'd been at Atlantis, Dan had been tricked into thinking that I had died. In his grief, he had destroyed his house. Now, he had a brand new house, one that had rooms for me and my mates to stay in, as well as two additional rooms for our potential future children. He'd also built a much larger dining room, a play room for children, and two living rooms.

"Your new bed was delivered," Dan informed me.

"Really?" I asked and started to head up the stairs.

"Auntie Jolie!" twin girls yelled as they raced out of the children's room near the stairway. Their noses still in the air, tracking my scent. They rushed over and slammed their little bodies into me.

Martin and Sharla walked out of the room and both hurried over to hug me.

Sharla pinched my arm. "You've been gone too long!" she chastised me, giving me her mom voice.

"I just talked to you two days ago," I reminded her.

"But I haven't seen you in over two weeks!" she said and pouted. "I missed your face."

"She does have a beautiful face," Martin said. Martin was Sharla's mate and my ex-boyfriend.

Sharla growled and pulled me into her arms. "No, I won't share her. You had her for years before I did," she said.

I chuckled and patted her back. "We need a girls' night."

"I don't know if I like the idea of you two going out together," Deryn said, eyeing Sharla.

"I'd be there to keep an eye on them," Leona said, draping an arm around both of us.

"That makes me even more nervous," Deryn said.

"Girls' night!" I shouted.

"Tonight?" Sharla asked, smile wide and eyes gleaming.

"Yes!" Leona and I agreed.

"Oh, boy," Dan said softly.

"You need a guard," Martin said.

"We can take Thor," Leona said and smirked.

"Not a chance!" I yelled at her.

"Who are we going to take then?" Sharla asked. "I'm not taking Martin. Leona can't take Thor. You can't take any of the princes."

"How about me?" Ezio asked, walking in from the dining

11

room. His copper hair glowed and his sapphire eyes focused on me.

"Ezio!" I breathed. Even mated to four gorgeous and powerful males, Ezio still affected me.

He hugged me and slid his cheek along mine. "Hello, Jolie."

"Why didn't you tell me you were in town?" I asked, inhaling his scent that reminded me of cologne.

"Sorry," he apologized and kissed my cheek.

"Great!" Dan said. "That settles that. Ezio will go out with the girls to protect them. Everyone's happy."

"I don't know about everyone," Deryn muttered.

I turned and arched a brow at him.

He smiled and pulled me away from Ezio to kiss me and nuzzle my neck. "I can't help being jealous."

"Moon Moon. I'm yours. We're mated," I reminded him.

"Yeah, but look at him," he whispered. "He looks like a god."

I burst into laughter and only stopped when Deryn nipped my neck.

"I'm sorry," I said, trying to contain my laughter. "But, you know I'm not one to be unfaithful."

"I know," he whispered, his hand snaking around my lower back to pull me closer to him. "I'm trying to work on my jealousy."

"As long as you're working on it, that's all I ask for."

"Come, let's eat," Dan said. He clapped a hand on his son's shoulder. "I need to speak to you after we eat."

Deryn nodded. "Okay."

We made our way into the dining room and took our seats. Dan and Deryn sat at the heads of the table. I sat to Deryn's right and Nico sat on my right. The table was set with a bunch of food and pitchers of tea and lemonade.

I reached for the lemonade, but Nico beat me to it, filling my glass for me.

"Thanks," I said and kissed his cheek.

Everyone filled their plates and ate, chatting about random topics. I listened and relaxed. This was what I had always wanted my life to be like. Surrounded by those I loved, enjoying life, and just being happy.

Nico set his hand on my thigh and rubbed his thumb across it slowly and gently.

I leaned my head against his shoulder for a moment while chewing. Our connection was so much stronger now. Apparently, trying to kill him had helped us. Who knew?

There was an explosion outside the house, so close that the dishes rattled on the table. Nico and Deryn wrapped their bodies around mine, protecting me in case anything came near us. The next second, all of the males except Fox and Martin were gone. Martin and Sharla each held one of their daughters and Fox was behind me.

"What is it?" I asked, trying to look outside.

"Shelter," Martin growled and spun around.

Sharla followed him, and Fox nudged me after the family.

I didn't want to go hide in the shelter. I wanted to find out what was going on.

"Once you're inside, I'll find out what's going on and—"

"All clear," Ezio said as he entered the house, saving me from going into the shelter. "Jolie, you should come outside."

I hurried out and came to a stop by Rhys. He linked our hands together, squeezing mine for reassurance.

"They caught me away from home," Johann gasped.

He had blood coating his shirt and dribbling from his chin.

"Mom?" Nico asked.

"She's at home. She is safe."

"Why come here?" Dan asked.

"I teleported to Nico," Johann explained.

"Katar is on his way," Rhys said.

Johann groaned, his eyes squeezing shut as he tensed from pain. "It's too late."

I dropped to my knees beside him. "Stop talking," I ordered him. I set my hands on his chest and opened my bond with Fox to begin healing him. His internal injuries were much worse than any of us knew. That's why he was giving up. He was bleeding internally and had several broken ribs and a pierced lung.

Johann set his hand on top of mine. "Take care of him. He's going to need all the help he can get to be king," he whispered.

"No," I rasped, tears welling in my eyes.

Fox knelt and ran his hand along Johann's chest and stomach. "He has extensive internal injuries," Fox told Nico.

"Dad," Nico whispered and knelt by him. "Who was it?"

"Dhampirs," Johann said. He looked at me. "Your dreams might be premonitions after all."

Shit. That was not what I wanted to hear. In my nightmares, my mates died.

Nico's body was beginning to glow. His fury and grief were beginning to consume him.

"Take care of each other," Johann whispered to Nico and gripped his hand. "Don't make the same mistakes I did."

"Dad," Nico whispered.

Johann took a big breath, held out a ring to Nico and then all of his remaining magic siphoned into it. Johann's body fell limp to the ground just as Katar came up.

Katar dropped next to Johann and set his hands on Johann's chest. "Dammit! No!"

Kara hugged Nico and whispered something in his ear, but Nico didn't seem to hear.

"I need to check on my people," he said as he slipped on his father's ring.

"Do you want me to—"

He disappeared before I could even finish my question, but luckily Fox had set his hand on Nico's shoulder and went with him, so at least he wasn't alone.

Rhys pulled me to my feet and hugged me. Johann hadn't

liked me much, but he was my father-in-law and he had been a good king. Plus, I could feel Nico's grief through our bond and it hurt me.

"Where are the dhampirs?" I asked Rhys, trying not to cry.

"Dead. He said he managed to kill them and then teleported here," Rhys whispered.

Dan knelt beside Katar, tears in his eyes as he stared at his dead friend.

CHAPTER 2

JOLIE

Rhys took me inside and gave me a warm mug of tea. I sipped on it silently, staring at the floor.

Johann was dead. Dhampirs had killed him. I couldn't let my mates die too.

"He just needs some time," Rhys said. "Fox will help him deal with his initial grief."

Shouldn't I feel worse about Johann's death? He was my father-in-law. But, he had said so many things to me.

"He's closed our bond," I whispered and rubbed at my chest.

Rhys nodded and rubbed my back. "He's doing it so you don't endure his grief."

"I should be helping him," I said.

"You will. For now, he needs to deal with it with his family and Fox. Your time to help him will come. You should still go out tonight," Rhys said.

"Really? You think I should still go out?" I asked.

He nodded. "Yes."

"Come on. Now's the perfect time to go out for a drink," Leona said with a wide smile.

"There's nothing for you to do right now," Rhys said. "I think it would be best if you went out with your friends."

"Are you sure?" I asked. It felt wrong to go out after such a tragedy.

Rhys nodded. "I'm sure."

"Okay," I agreed with a sigh.

"Ezio!" Sharla called.

"Yes?" he asked, walking down the stairs.

"You ready to take us out?" she asked him.

He looked at me a moment and then said, "Yeah."

"Keep a close eye on them," Rhys ordered Ezio.

Ezio glared at him, but said nothing.

I set my tea down and kissed Rhys. "Love you."

He rested his hand on my cheek and smiled. "I love you, too."

Ezio drove us to Leona's favorite bar. It was a decent sized place with a dance area and served drinks with plenty of alcohol for the cost. It also usually had patrons around our age and good music. She had forced my mates and I to go several times since she'd arrived in Jinla.

Leona sauntered up to the bar, smiling at Rowdy, the owner and bartender.

"Hello, gorgeous," Rowdy greeted her. He looked at me and Sharla. "You brought more beautiful women for me to meet?"

I rolled my eyes. With Leona around, men forgot about any other women with her. I had met Rowdy multiple times, but he only remembered Leona.

"They heard you had the best drinks in town, and we desperately needed a girls' night," Leona told him.

He picked up a silver shaker and flipped it around a few times before catching it. "What are you girls having?"

"Three of your special drinks," Leona said.

"I'm going to find a dark corner to stand guard in," Ezio said, his breath stirring my hair.

"Okay," I said. "Sorry you were relegated to babysitting us."

He smirked and kissed my cheek. "I'll babysit you anytime you want."

I laughed and joined Sharla and Leona on barstools at the bar.

"You good?" Leona asked.

I nodded. "Ezio's making himself scarce so we can enjoy our night."

Sharla smirked. "He's still got a thing for you."

"He also knows he can't have me and he respects me enough not to really try anything," I said. And, it was true. He may flirt on occasion, but he wouldn't actually try anything. One, he knew I would turn him down. Two, he didn't really want to deal with fighting my four mates.

"Could you stop hogging all the hot guys?" Leona asked me with fake irritation, her brows furrowed. "Do you know how hard it is to find a single guy who isn't in love with you?"

Sharla tossed back her head and laughed.

"Stop looking at werewolves and you'll find some," I teased.

"I saw clips from the Summit. You've got all the hottest guys in love with you," Leona said. "If I didn't know your siren abilities were locked back then, I'd assume you lured them somehow."

I rolled my eyes at her. "You know that's not what happened."

"I know. You're just too damn likable!" she said and sighed. "You were as a kid, too. I wanted to hate you, but you were just too nice and too much fun."

I smiled triumphantly. "Say it."

"I love you," she said. Then grumbled, "Jerk."

Sharla and I laughed loudly, but were cut off when a guy draped his arms around Sharla and my shoulders.

"What can I buy you beautiful ladies?" he asked.

"Some space?" Sharla asked and pushed his arm off her shoulder.

"Oh, don't be like that," he said and moved closer to me.

"We'll pass, thanks," I said and smiled sweetly. "We're on a no-guy type of night."

"Just your luck, I'm a yes-guy type," he smirked, thinking he was clever.

"The ladies have been nice and now I'll be rude. Move the fuck on," Ezio growled.

I turned, finally able to catch a glimpse of the guy now that his arm was gone. He was cute, middle-aged, and not cowed by Ezio at all.

"I thought this was a no-guy night?" he asked me.

"He's the muscle," I said. "He doesn't count."

"Plus, she's already tasted that several times," Leona whispered around her drink.

I glared at her.

Rowdy slid my drink to me. "Here you go."

"Thanks!" I said and took a big gulp. It was fruity, sweet, and amazing.

"Leave the girls alone," Ezio said. "Now."

"Whatever. These old hoes aren't that pretty anyway," the man grumbled.

Before I could stop him, Ezio punched the guy. The guy fell to the ground, unconscious.

Leona cheered and Sharla clapped.

"Ezio," I whispered, my mouth agape. He very rarely lost control.

He looked at me, and his cheeks reddened slightly. "What?"

I shook my head, mouth still open, but didn't respond.

"I don't care if you're mine or not. I'm not letting some asshat disrespect you. Your mates wouldn't let him, and I'm their stand in."

"I bet he'd stand in for other things while your mates are gone," Sharla whispered in my ear.

"Shut up," I growled at her. I looked at Leona. "You're a bad influence on her. I shouldn't let you two hang out anymore."

Leona pouted, and Sharla cackled loudly.

"I'll be back," Ezio said as he carried the unconscious guy away from us.

"Another drink," I ordered Rowdy. He looked at my full glass, and then his eyes widened when I downed it in two gulps.

We waited until Ezio was back inside and at his post, leaning against the far wall, before we made our way to the dance floor. Sharla, Leona, and I danced along to the music, the alcohol flowing heavily within our systems now.

A guy tried to dance with Sharla, but Leona and I maneuvered between him and her, dancing right up against her. He took the hint and left.

"You're the princess!" a male voice gasped to my right.

I turned and eyed the guy who didn't look old enough to be in the bar, especially with such wide doe eyes.

"Yeah?" I said, unsure why it mattered.

He bowed his head slightly. "I'm Steven, a friend of Mawrth's. I'm a dragon," he said.

Mawrth and I weren't exactly on good terms, so I narrowed my eyes. "Nice to meet you," I said.

"Um, is Prince Rhys here? I actually need to talk to him about something," he looked around, searching for him.

"No, he's not here right now. Do you want to tell me so I can tell him? Or you can give me a number, and I'll have him contact you." His hands were shaking slightly, which made me nervous.

I looked at Ezio and once our eyes met, he headed my way, moving through people easily.

"Um, I'd like to tell him. It's sort of urgent and dangerous," he said.

"Dangerous for who?" I asked, my body tensing. I could fight if I needed to, but I didn't want any bystanders getting mixed up in it. Or Leona and Sharla.

"Everything okay?" Ezio asked, stopping by me.

Steven's mouth dropped open. "You're Ezio!" he said, his eyes sparkling.

Looked like Ezio had a fan.

"Yeah. Who are you?" Ezio asked.

"He said he has a message for Rhys and it's urgent and dangerous," I told Ezio.

Ezio's body tensed just as mine had. "Why don't we talk about this outside?" Ezio suggested.

"Okay," Steven said. He gave me a smile and then walked ahead of Ezio out of the bar.

"That was weird," Leona whispered behind me, her mouth right by my ear.

I spun around, ready to punch her before I caught myself and tried to calm my now racing heart. "Dammit! Don't do that."

She smirked and then it slipped away. "What could he want?"

"It was a weird interaction," Sharla said, standing beside Leona. "He seemed to idolize you and Ezio."

"I'm sorry. My business always ruins our fun," I grumbled.

Sharla patted my shoulder. "Let's get another—"

Sharla's words were cut off as a huge explosion went off outside of the bar, breaking the glass windows and shaking the ground.

"Ezio!" I screamed, racing around the panicked bar patrons, most having ducked down and covered their heads. I didn't bother waiting to see if Sharla and Leona would follow. They could protect themselves. My only concern was Ezio.

I jumped through the broken front window and searched the street for him. There was a smoking hole in the center of the street, I guessed that was where the bomb had detonated.

"Ezio!" I screamed, my ears still ringing from the blast.

Wind from above pushed down at me. I jerked my gaze up and glared at the dragon hovering there. It had to be Steven, since they'd just stepped outside together. In his paw, I saw Ezio's unconscious body.

I roared and shifted into my dragon form, leaping up into the air before I'd fully shifted. Teeth bared, I flew at the dragon, ready to tear him to pieces and get Ezio back.

He backed up, eyes wide with panic, and then shifted back to human form and dropped to the ground, holding Ezio in his arms.

I landed, but stayed in my dragon form, snarling and growling at him.

He set Ezio on the ground. "I grabbed him and tried to get clear of the bomb, but he got hit by some debris," he told me. He took several steps away and raised his hands, palms out.

I shifted back to human form and knelt by Ezio. "Ezio," I said, trying to keep myself calm. "I need you to wake up. Someone could hurt me." I wasn't actually worried about myself, but hoped it might incentivize him to wake up.

He had several cuts that were already healing, but nothing that should have knocked him unconscious. I lifted his head gingerly, feeling around it for a lump or blood, but found none.

"He'll wake up in a few minutes," a deep voice said.

I spun around, crouched over Ezio's body and snarled, my teeth lengthening and thickening into a wolf's fangs.

He looked like a cross between Nico and Brayden. In his hand he held a metal staff with a silver glowing orb on the end of it. Mage.

I tugged on my bond with Nico, but he'd shut it down so tightly that I wasn't sure if he could feel it. I tugged on my other three bonds, hoping they would all come.

"Who are you and what the fuck do you want?" I snarled.

He smirked. "You don't know who I am? Why, is Daddy dearest keeping secrets?"

"I don't know you or your dad," I said. "Why did you hurt Ezio? What do you want?"

"Sweet, sweet, Jolie," he said, beginning a slow walk around me. "You're so naïve. My brothers and father must really be keeping a lid on my existence. It's sad really because if you'd been prepared, you could have prevented this."

He lunged for me, and I covered my body in scales and grew wolf claws. Nico popped into existence at my side and put a shield up, which his weird doppleganger leapt away from before touching.

Nico held his staff and glared at the guy. "Are you hurt, love?"

"No, but he knocked Ezio out somehow. There was an explosion and Ezio won't wake up," I said.

"He'll be fine," Nico assured me, still not taking his eyes off of the attacker.

"Brother!" the guy said and smiled wide. "I thought provoking your mate might force you to make an appearance."

Brother? He really was related to Nico.

Nico held his glare a moment longer and then turned to face me. His eyes were red, from crying no doubt, and glimmered with fury. "Can you teleport to the den?" he asked me.

I set my hand on his cheek and said, "I'm not leaving you."

He smiled and turned his head to kiss my palm. "I wasn't suggesting you leave me. I just need to know."

I nodded. "Yes."

"Where are the girls?" he asked.

"Inside the bar," I answered, keeping a wary eye on Nico's brother who stood with his arms folded, tapping his foot, and glaring at us.

"Sharla! Leona!" Nico yelled. "Here, please."

Both ran from the bar to dash inside Nico's shield. Sharla knelt at Ezio's side and inspected him.

"You have to talk to me eventually," Nico's brother said. "I won't stop until you do."

"Don't test me, Klaus. Have you spoken to your brother?" Nico asked, his lip twitching as he held in a snarl.

"Brayden?" Klaus asked.

Nico nodded.

I turned and stared at Nico in shock. Brayden was his brother? He hadn't told me that! Why was he keeping secrets? What the hell!

"No. Why? What did he do this time?" Klaus asked.

"He's on my kill list," Nico told him. "He tried to steal my mate and forced her to forget me."

Klaus's eyes widened. "He was the one trying to steal the siren throne?"

Nico nodded.

Klaus looked at me. "You're the siren princess?"

I nodded.

He sighed and said, "I'm sorry. I wasn't going to hurt her. I didn't realize it was you that was involved. Had I known, I wouldn't have frightened your mate."

"What do you want?" I asked him.

Klaus ignored me, focused on Nico. "I need to talk to you, Nico. There are things happening and—"

Nico cut him off. "I don't have time for this. Dad's dead. I've got shit to do."

"What?" Klaus asked, his face void of emotion and his tone neutral.

"Dhampirs killed him," Nico said and cleared his throat as emotions built in him.

"When?" Klaus asked.

"Today," I answered and slipped my hand in Nico's.

"I'll find you again later," Klaus said. He looked at me and then met Nico's glare. "Keep her close."

He disappeared the next instant.

"Teleport us to the den," Nico ordered me.

"Wait!" Steven yelled. "I need to speak to the prince!"

Nico dropped the shield and staggered forward a bit. I stood before him, letting him lean on me in a way that appeared he was simply cuddling me and kept him from looking weak.

"Come with us," I told Steven. "If you try anything, I'll kill you."

His eyes widened and he nodded before jogging over to us.

"Everyone put a hand on each other. Steven, pick up Ezio," I said.

Everyone obeyed and I teleported us to the den, just outside of Dan's house. Dan threw open the door and growled, eyes fixed on Ezio.

"Easy," I ordered Dan. "Let us explain everything."

"You're bleeding," Dan growled.

I was?

"It's a superficial wound," Nico said. "It should stop bleeding in a moment."

"Why are you so weak?" I asked him softly.

"Used a lot of power too quickly just before you summoned me," he explained.

"Where are the rest of the guys?" I asked.

"Helping my people prepare for my father's funeral," Nico said.

"Dan, can you take Nico to our room?" I asked.

Nico started to object, but Dan put his arm around Nico's waist and pulled Nico's arm around his shoulders. "Don't argue with your mate. She's got that crazed look in her eye," Dan whispered.

Thor stepped out of the house, glaring at Steven.

"Thor, can you take Ezio inside?" I asked.

I tugged on Rhys's bond and he tugged back.

Thor took Ezio and frowned. "What happened?"

"Mage," I said. "Nico said he's fine and will wake up soon."

Thor nodded and left.

"Rhys is on his way," I told Steven. "You can wait in the dining room until he arrives."

Steven nodded and followed me inside.

Martin stood from the couch and hugged Sharla.

After getting Steven to the dining room, I returned to Martin and Sharla. "I'm sorry," I whispered and looked at my feet. "I didn't mean to put your mate in danger."

"It wasn't your fault," Sharla said.

"Just being around me is dangerous," I said.

Martin pulled me into a hug. "It's alright."

"We're good?" I asked as I rubbed my face on his shirt.

He rubbed the center of my back and nodded against my hair. "Yeah."

"What's going on?" Rhys asked as he entered the house.

I pulled away from Martin and rubbed a hand down my face. I was so tired. I hadn't realized it until now. "A friend of Mawrth's said he has to tell you something and it's dangerous," I explained. "He's in the dining room."

"What happened?" Rhys asked, his voice a deep growl as he touched the side of my head.

"Talk to him first. Then, I'll tell you," I said. I rubbed a hand down my face again.

"Go to our room," Rhys whispered and kissed my cheek. "I'll be up as soon as I'm done with him."

I nodded and then scowled as I looked around the room. "Where's Leona?"

"She snuck off with Thor somewhere," Sharla said and smiled. "I doubt you'll see her the rest of the night."

I laughed and shook my head as I made my way up to the second floor and then to the room we used while staying at the werewolf den. Nico lay on the bed, still clothed, but asleep.

As quietly as possible, I climbed into bed with him. He stirred slightly, slid an arm beneath my pillow, and then spooned himself around me. Within a minute, I was fast asleep.

CHAPTER 3

JOLIE

Johann's funeral was short and emotional. Mages burned the bodies of their dead, so my four mates and I stood and waited until his body was gone. Nico stayed longer to take care of some stuff, but sent us away.

Back at the house, Deryn turned on a movie, and pulled me down onto his lap. He nuzzled my neck and asked, "What's going on in that beautiful head of yours?"

"Nico never told me he has brothers," I whispered. "He never told me Brayden is his brother."

Deryn's head snapped up. "Trident Douche?"

I nodded.

"He didn't tell us that. Are you sure he's—"

"He confirmed it when talking to his *other* brother," I said. I took a deep breath and whispered, "It made me realize that there is a lot I still don't know about you guys. I'm a shit mate."

His arms tightened around me. "No, you're not. We're just very secretive. It comes from years of training by our parents. We don't mean to keep secrets or things from you."

I paused the movie since we weren't watching it anyway and straddled him so I could fully face him. "Tell me something about you that I don't know," I requested.

He thought about it and asked, "Have I ever told you about my mom?"

"No," I said, focusing intently on him. I had wanted to ask about her before, but was worried it was a heartbreaking story and didn't want to upset him or Dan.

"Mom was full of fire. She was always working on something and was adamant that things got done, if she believed in them. Dad and Mom became mates when they were sixteen. Her parents were pissed, but Mom put her foot down and told them two more years didn't matter. She loved Dad and that's what was important. When Dad became alpha, they praised their match, which irked my mother so much.

"One day there was an attack on the den. Vampires. Mom didn't want to let everyone else fight while she just sat back and worried. You remind me of her a lot, actually. Anyway, she went out of the house to help fight and protect the weaker wolves in the pack. The vampires ganged up on her, and before Dad or I could get to her, they killed her. Dad went crazy, murdering everything he saw. I was lucky enough to get the wolves away, so there were no casualties on our side. Dad mourned her for months, probably longer than that to be honest, but that's what I saw."

"How old were you when she died?" I asked softly, linking our hands.

"Eighteen," he said. "Dad keeps a smile on his face, and I know the pain isn't as bad for him now, but to this day, I hear him talking to her."

I couldn't imagine losing a mate after so long. The pain I felt when our bonds were severed was torture enough, but for them to actually die...

"Dad loves you, Jolie. You're the daughter he never had. You saw it the day we came back from Atlantis. He keeps pushing me in training and is pushing the rest of the pack as well, preparing for war. He told me that if someone steals you again, he's going to be ready to 'knock their fucking doors down and take you back.'"

Tears burned in my eyes, threatening to fall, but I blinked them back. Dan was amazing, and I needed to do something for him. To show how much I appreciated him.

Deryn pulled me forward, hugging me tightly, and rested his forehead on my shoulder. "That's why I hate that you put yourself in danger so much. I can't lose you, too. I can't watch you die, while I'm unable to help you. But, you keep getting hurt. You keep rushing into things. I love you, Jolie. I love you more than anything else in the world."

I snuggled closer to him and whispered, "I love you too, Moon Moon."

He chuckled and kissed the side of my neck. "Are you hungry?"

"Just a bit more cuddling?" I requested.

He fell to his side, pulling me with him, and we quickly tangled our legs together. I let him wrap the top half of my body up in his arms. We lay like that for who knows how long, only separating when Nico cleared his throat.

"I, uh, sorry, but can I borrow her?" Nico asked, rubbing the back of his neck.

I stood, and Deryn smiled.

"You know you don't have to ask," Deryn said.

Nico nodded, linked our hands and teleported us to his bedroom.

"What's up?" I asked him. "How are you holding up?"

He ran a hand through his disheveled hair, and I noticed the bags beneath his eyes. "There's so much to deal with during this transition period," he said. "It's just...a lot."

"What do you need from me?" I asked, stepping closer to him. "How can I help?"

He smiled down at me and pressed his forehead to mine. "Honestly, I just wanted to lie with you a bit."

I tugged his hand and climbed onto the bed. He took his shoes off and climbed on after me. I waited until he laid down on his back before snuggling up against his side and resting my head on his chest.

"I love you, Nico."

He wrapped one arm around my side and squeezed. "I love you, too."

"Do you want me to play with your hair until you fall asleep?" I asked, already reaching up.

He snuggled closer to me with a happy smile and nodded.

I ran my fingers through his hair, my fingertips feeling along his scalp as I did. It wasn't long before he was asleep and softly snoring. I tried to climb out of the bed, but his hand snatched out and grabbed my wrist. "Please...don't leave," he whispered, his eyes fluttering open.

I hurriedly climbed back onto the bed and snuggled into him. "Okay," I said. "I'll stay with you as long as you want me to."

"Forever," he whispered. "Forever sounds good."

"Forever and ever," I whispered back.

"I'M WHAT?" I SCREECHED, STARING AT NICO IN DISBELIEF. WE'D woken up the next morning and the bags beneath his eyes were thankfully gone now.

"You're Queen of the Mages," Nico said again. "Since I'm King now and you're my mate..."

"Oh," I breathed.

He chuckled and said, "It's not the end of the world. There really isn't that much that you need to do."

"I just..." I didn't finish the sentence. I was going to say I hadn't planned for this to happen so soon, but Nico hadn't planned for this either. His father being murdered is what caused it.

He wrapped his arms around me and said, "I know. It's going to be okay. We'll get through this together, right?"

I nodded, turned, and smiled at him. "Right. What do you need me to do?" I asked.

"Tomorrow, I need you to come with me to speak with the elders of the mages and start learning about my race," he said. "There's a lot that you don't know, and I want you to be prepared."

"Nico, why didn't you tell me that you had siblings? Or that Brayden was your brother?" I asked him, stepping out of his hold.

He sighed and rubbed the back of his neck. "I didn't know until we were restoring your memories. I felt his magic and the bond we shared then. He's my half-brother and Dad never told me about him. I confronted Dad when we returned, and he confirmed that I have not one or two, but six half-siblings."

Six? Wolfsbane! That was a lot of unknown siblings.

"And why didn't he tell you before?" I asked.

"Because he'd left on not-so-good terms with the women and had only stuck with me and my mother. So, most of the women hate me and my mother," he explained.

"You don't think one of them could be responsible—"

"It's a possibility," he said with a nod. "Especially if Brayden hooked up with Justina. She is a dhampir, after all."

If they'd joined forces, it could be a very, very bad thing for us.

"Hey, stop fretting about the future. We're going to just focus on today and what needs to get accomplished now. Right?" he said.

I nodded and stepped into his arms. "You are lucky you're pretty," I mumbled into his chest.

He laughed, a true laugh, and I felt my heart soar. It was the first time I'd heard that type of laugh in a week at least.

"He is rather pretty," Deryn teased from the doorway.

"What's up?" Nico asked him, turning away from me.

"Just came to get you for food," Deryn said.

I finished getting ready and then followed them to the dining room where a huge feast was ready.

Leona sat with Thor beside her, their heads close together, and adorable smirks on their faces. They were an adorable couple. Now that they were officially dating, Thor had been at our house almost every night.

"What's the plan for today?" I asked as I sat.

"I'm hiding at the house today," Nico said, sitting on my right. "I need some decompression time."

"Actually, I was hoping you would come with me today," Thor said as he faced me.

"Me?" I asked, looking at Leona who was piling her plate with food.

"I'm going to visit my pack with Martin. We thought you might want to go with us," Thor said.

"Your pack!" I screeched, excitement coursing through me. "I haven't seen them in years!"

"I'm coming, if you go," Deryn said.

"She's not in any danger with my pack," Thor said and I could tell he was holding back an eye roll.

"I didn't suggest she would be. I just want to meet your alpha and talk to some of the wolves there," Deryn explained.

"Trying to find out if I'm hiding secrets?" I asked.

He kissed my cheek and took the seat on my left. "No, gorgeous. I just want to find out more about the pack and your involvement."

Thor and I exchanged a look that let me know I wasn't the only one not buying it. Whatever his reason, I had nothing to hide.

"I'm sure Alpha would love to meet you. He'd always said he'd love to meet whoever could handle me as a mate," I said.

Thor chuckled and began filling his plate.

"When are you going?" Deryn asked.

"In about three hours," Thor answered. "Martin is finishing up some work and then he'll swing by to pick us up."

"Sounds great!" I said.

After eating, I went to Fox's room and lay with him on the floor. He gently stroked his fingertips up and down my arm, his eyes focused on the ceiling above us, and his thoughts somewhere unknown.

"What's up?" I asked him. "You're rarely quiet and so serious."

"Just thinking about your dreams," he whispered.

I rolled onto my side and rested my head on his chest, wrapping my arms around his torso. "I won't let it come true," I whispered.

He kissed the top of my head and whispered, "As long as you are safe, that's all that matters."

"No. I don't...can't live without you. I need you all," I said, tightening my grip.

"We're working on making ourselves stronger. You should summon your new friends soon. So you can work out whatever deals you may need before a time of crisis," Fox said.

He was referring to the two magical tattoos now on my forearms. One was of a fox, a kitsune to be exact, named Nar. The second was of a unicorn and had been given to me by my mother.

"I'll do that this weekend," I promised.

"I love you, Jolie. I love you more than I thought was possible to love someone. Nico's father dying reminded us that we aren't invincible. And, that we must be as strong as possible to keep you safe. We've almost lost you a couple of times, and I won't let it happen again. When I see Justina, I'm going to tear out her heart and shove it down her throat."

Fox's eyes were bright with power and his body was tight, coiled for a fight. I had never heard him say such threatening things before. I was shocked and sadly, smug that it was because of me.

"When you didn't remember us at Atlantis, I was furious. It hurt so much to have you look at us like strangers again, to not see the love you usually show when you look at us. Plus, you had shut down our bonds so tightly I couldn't feel you. It was terrible."

I squeezed him. "I'm sorry. I know I've caused you a lot of trouble since we met."

He chuckled. "That's an understatement. But, the thing is, I wouldn't trade a moment of it. Having you in my life is worth any amount of trouble you might bring."

"You're so sweet," I whispered, leaned up, and kissed him.

"How long until you have to go?" he asked and kissed me again, his hand roaming up my side.

"We have at least an hour," I said in a breathy voice, my lower body already warming in anticipation.

He sighed. "Only an hour? I shall have to make it a worthy hour then."

He flipped us over and with me pinned beneath him, he kissed me deeply, pressing his lower body into mine and making me all too aware how happy he was to be there. When we had mated, it had been incredibly passionate and when the bond snapped into place, it was bordering on overwhelming. Ever since the mating, sex between us had been incredible. Not to say that it was in anyway unenjoyable before, but Fox was usually more sensual than sexual overall. Lately our love making had been so intensely passionate, my mind refused to process that this was the same man. Fox undressed me slowly, sensually, but with a feverish need edging into each of his motions. He kissed along each piece of skin as he exposed it, licking and teasing my naked body as he stripped me down. As he came to my pert nipple, he flicked his tongue over it teasingly then took it into his mouth and sucked hard on the sensitive peak. I moaned and arched up into his skilled touch.

"Are you too worked up for this much foreplay?" He asked as

he slid two fingers deep inside of me, his eyes widening when he felt how very wet I already was.

"Yes," I whispered, arching as his fingers began to slide out of me.

"Damn, baby, you are supposed to tell us when you are this wet and ready."

He stood in one smooth motion, making me reach for him and start to beg him to come back to the bed. I lost all my words as his shirt fell to the floor and his upper body was revealed. As his hands went to the top button of his pants I slid my fingers down my body and began touching myself while he undressed. His eyes tracked my movements and I watched his body spasm against his still closed zipper. I continued to work that oh so sensitive nub while his pants fell to the floor next to his shirt. He was suddenly on top of me, kissing down my throat and collarbone.

I kept working that sweet spot at the top of my center even as he slid his erection within me. He filled me and stretched me and made my body spasm around him with that initial thrust. One thrust, two, three, and he found a rhythm. We both moaned at the same time. I could feel the orgasm building both from where my fingers still teased my body and the deep strokes of Fox as he pushed in and out of me.

"Damn, Jolie! You haven't been this wet in a long time." He . began to thrust into me harder and faster and the orgasm broke over me in a wave of dizzying heat and release. And still he pushed into me. As the orgasm subsided I tapped him on the shoulder with a devious smile. He pulled out slowly and rolled to his back beside me, still rock hard and waiting for his own release.

I rolled to my knees and kissed him deeply, then straddled his hips and lowered myself over him, blissfully enjoying each inch as his body was sheathed inside mine. I began to rotate my hips in a slow rise and fall. It only took him a bare minute to catch the rhythm of my hips and match it with his own slow and even strokes. I knew he was close and so was I but I wanted to make the moment last, as we only had an hour to enjoy one another's company. I leaned back until he almost slipped out of me, then rode forward across his body and rocked my hips back and forth over his shaft while I kissed him deeply.

"Now. Please, Fox. Now. I'm so close."

"Me too, Jolie."

I felt his hips arc into me as I rode his body down and suddenly we were both crashing over that glimmering edge. I fell forward into his arms and we both lay there, panting as we tried to catch our breath and find feeling in our limbs again. It may have been a short hour but we were both sated.

CHAPTER 4

JOLIE

I sat in the front passenger seat while Martin drove. Deryn and Thor sat in the back seats, talking quietly, too quietly for me to hear.

"Are you excited?" Martin asked.

I nodded, thinking about Abraham, the alpha. "I haven't seen Abraham since I moved out of my dad's, er, step-dad's house."

"He's always asking about you."

"He was such a great alpha," I said. "I am lucky to have been part of your pack."

"You like him better than my dad?" Deryn asked.

I spun and stared at him. "What? I didn't say that."

"You talk about him in an almost reverent tone," he said.

"He was my first alpha and he treated me like one of them," I said. "He made me feel wanted when I was unwanted at home."

"You didn't answer my question," Deryn pointed out.

"I don't like one more than the other. I like them differently," I said.

"How?" Deryn asked.

"Abraham was like my cool uncle. Dan is like the father I always wanted," I said. "Not sure if that makes sense."

Deryn nodded and relaxed back in his seat. "Yeah, it makes sense."

I was glad, because I didn't really want to discuss it anymore. It wasn't fair to ask who I liked more. That was like asking a parent who their favorite child was. Or asking the child who their favorite parent was. Or asking who my favorite mate was.

We entered the pack's compound and people rushed out of their houses to come see us. There were many I had never seen before, but so many I knew were still there.

I climbed out of the SUV and was immediately inundated with hugs and cheek kisses. I was in the middle of a group of girls I'd known in high school when Abraham stopped before me.

I turned to face him fully and smiled up at him. "Alpha," I whispered and bowed my head respectfully.

He tilted my face up and tapped the bloodstones. "Mated?"

"She is," Deryn said.

All eyes turned to him. Deryn stood a bit away from us, his posture relaxed, but his eyes hard as he focused on Abraham.

Abraham turned to face him and asked, "You're one of her mates?"

Deryn nodded. "I am."

"I suppose he might be alpha enough for you," Abraham said. "Though, I always rooted for Ezio."

Deryn's lip twitched as he held back a snarl.

"Alpha," I said in a reprimanding tone.

Abraham turned and embraced me. "I've missed you, child."

I hugged him back and rubbed my face on his shirt, a habit I still couldn't break. "I missed you, too."

He pushed me back and turned to face Deryn. "You came to speak with me?"

Deryn nodded. "Privately, please."

"This way," Abraham said and waved Deryn towards his

house. Deryn turned towards me and opened his mouth, but Abraham cut him off. "She's safer here than with any other pack. This is *her* pack."

Deryn scowled. "She's not—"

"She's ours," Molly, a shorter female werewolf with a shaved head said and wrapped her arm around my waist. "None here would harm her."

"Come on, let's go hunt!" Linus called and several shouted in approval.

"No," Deryn growled. His growl and word were laced with command and it caused everyone to still. "I won't allow her to hunt with you."

I scowled. "Deryn, I hunted with them for years."

"You know we wouldn't let anything happen to her," Thor said and walked to stand behind me with Martin on his right.

"I can't risk it. Jolie, please stay within the compound," Deryn ordered. He turned and walked into the house without another word.

"What the hell was that about?" I asked Thor, looking up at him.

He was scowling and looking at the house Deryn had gone in to. "I don't know."

"Well, if we can't hunt, let's play!" Linus said, not missing a beat.

I walked to Linus, hugged him, and then slapped his arm and yelled, "You're it!" as I ran away.

The pack scattered, some turning into wolves while most stayed human. The pack ran about the compound, swerving around buildings and dodging the person who was *it*. With over fifty people, the game became a squealing and laugher-filled event. Not once did someone get mad or growl about being tagged. That was one of the biggest reasons I loved this pack. Everyone got along. Abraham created a sense of belonging, and we all genuinely enjoyed being around each other. Sure, there were bumps in the road or drama, but they were rare occurrences.

I ducked out of Linus's reach as he tried to tag me, laughing as he chased me around a building. I ran into Deryn, and Linus ran into me.

Linus staggered back, his head bowed. "Sorry." I could smell the fear wafting around him.

I grabbed Linus and tugged him around Deryn. "Hurry!" I yelled.

Linus ran after me and Deryn stared at me with a scowl.

"Deryn's it!" I yelled, finally releasing Linus's hand now that he was away from Deryn and the scent of his fear was gone.

Deryn exhaled, letting his head drop forward a moment, and then he raised it with a full smile in place and raced after me.

I screamed and dodged around Linus and then Thor who was closest. Deryn tagged Thor. "Thor's it!" he yelled.

Thor chuckled and ran after one of the other pack members who was closest. He chased after a toddler, but then swerved around the toddler to tag an adult. We liked the kids to be involved, but tried not to make them the targets so they could just enjoy the chase.

Deryn slid his hands around my waist and pulled me back roughly against the front of his body, stopping me from running. "You look so beautiful right now," he whispered. "Seeing you with your face lit up with a smile and enjoying yourself with wolves is a definite turn on."

I pushed away from him and kissed his cheek. "You can be turned on later. I can't lose!"

Martin raced towards me, and I ran away from him. A big grey wolf stepped out in front of me, and I tripped over him, landing on my butt next to him.

He growled a moment and then nuzzled my cheek.

"Sorry," I whispered and rubbed at my sore butt as I stood.

The wolf shifted, and I immediately threw my arms around

the old man. He'd become fully grey while I was away, but there was no doubt that it was Peter, the second-in-command of the pack.

"Peter!" I squealed as I hugged him.

He hugged me back and chuckled. "Hello, troublesome human."

"I'm not human," I said when we separated.

He winked. "You'll always be the troublesome human girl I chased out of my gardens."

Deryn had stopped, standing several feet away from us.

"Peter, meet one of my mates, Deryn. Deryn, this is the second of the pack, Peter."

Deryn stepped forward and shook hands with Peter. "Nice to meet you."

Peter bowed his head. "Nice to meet you, too. I hope Jolie's not too much trouble for you."

"She's definitely a handful," Deryn said with a smirk, and draped his arm around my shoulders.

"That she is," Peter agreed and chuckled at my frown.

"So, you came to learn a bit more about Jolie's past with us?" Peter asked.

Deryn nodded. "Yes."

"She's quite a girl," Peter said, making me blush. "Take care of her, understand? I don't want to hear anymore sad news related to her."

Peter pinched the tip of my nose, smiled, and then shifted back into wolf form and trotted away.

"They really love you here," Deryn said.

"Are you surprised?" I asked, looking up at him.

He smirked. "No, but it is shocking to see a werewolf pack so readily accept a non-werewolf into it."

"It surprised me when I was younger, too," I admitted. I pulled Deryn to a nearby porch and sat on it with my legs dangling over the edge. "The first time Martin brought me to meet everyone, I was terrified. I thought they were going to eat me. I mean, I knew many of them from school, but I didn't know what they would be like here. As soon as Martin introduced me to Abraham, he pulled me into a hug, kissed the top of my head, and told me I was always welcome to come. I cried a bit, but honestly, they saved me. I was so broken from the vampire father who raised me and abused me, I'm not sure what type of person I would have turned out to be if Abraham hadn't brought me into the pack."

"He told me a bit about how you were in the beginning," Deryn said. "I'm sorry you had to endure so much as a child."

I kicked my legs back and forth and smiled. "It's okay. It made me who I am and whatever the path, it led me to you."

He bent and kissed me. "I love you, Jolie."

"I love you, too. But, I don't understand why you wouldn't let me go hunt," I said.

He sighed. "I didn't want you to go off somewhere and possibly get into danger while I was talking with Abraham."

"Thor and Martin would protect me," I reminded him.

"Yes, but it's not their job," he said.

"As my friends, it is," I countered.

"I'm sorry. I wasn't trying to be a rude jerk earlier."

"Can we go hunt now?" I asked. "Since you outrank them all, you should be fine hunting with them, right?"

He nodded. "Yes."

"Hunt!" I yelled and jumped down from the porch.

Several people yelled and others howled, and within a minute, most of the pack was waiting before me.

"Hunt!" I yelled again.

Deryn shifted, and I climbed onto his back. "Martin, lead the way!" I said.

Martin, and the rest who weren't already in wolf form shifted, and then Martin howled. Everyone, including Deryn, howled in response and the hairs on my arms stood up. Martin ran towards the trees and Deryn followed. Thor ran on our right, and I smiled over at him. He let his tongue loll out the side of his mouth as he ran, and yipped happily.

Into the trees we ran, and I hunkered down on Deryn's back, gripping his furred neck and holding on with my legs. He ran in the center of the pack, letting others take charge of the hunt.

There was some yipping, and then I saw the herd of deer ahead. Deryn slowed a bit more, letting more of the pack race past him to take the deer down. The first deer was taken down, and Deryn slowed to a stop.

I patted his shoulder and then lay on him fully and sighed. "Wolf fur is so soft and warm," I purred.

He lay down, carefully, so I didn't fall off his back, and huffed softly.

"Thank you, for coming hunting with us," I whispered.

Cinnamon, a brown colored wolf, trotted towards us with blood on her muzzle. She yipped at me and dropped the front half of her body down and wagged her tail. I darted off of Deryn and tackled her. She rolled with me and nipped at my hands and arms, but never hard enough to draw blood. We stopped rolling and squared off, me standing and her in a playful bow.

Deryn growled softly.

"She's not going to hurt me," I told her. "Cinnamon and I have known each other since junior high. Right, Cinn?"

Cinnamon yipped and stood on her back legs, letting her front paws rest on my shoulders as she licked my face.

"I missed you, too," I whispered and hugged her.

Deryn shifted into his human form. "This isn't normal," Deryn said softly. "I've never seen a wolf pack act like this."

"Just because it's not normal for you, doesn't mean it's not—"

"I don't mean just my pack. I've visited dozens of packs and spent weeks with them. I've seen them interact with humans who had married into the pack. None of them accepted the human like they accept you. This pack treats you like a pup. No, not a pup… I don't know! They treat you unlike anything I've seen!" Deryn yelled.

Cinnamon dropped down to all four feet and faced him. She tilted her head and yipped at him.

"She's not pack, though," Deryn said. "I appreciate the sentiment, but she's not in your pack by marking or connected through a mate."

Cinnamon yipped again.

Deryn's brows furrowed. "She…what?"

"I had a temporary mark," I answered, guessing what they were talking about. "Abraham marked me when I started coming around and then removed it when I turned eighteen."

"Why?"

"To protect me, I think, but it didn't help since my dad was a vampire," I explained.

Deryn's brows were so deeply furrowed, I worried he would have permanent lines. "He marked you, but then removed it? You were part of this pack, but then left it. Now, you're part of my pack."

"Permanently," I said with a wide smile.

He looked up and the frown disappeared, replaced by a wide smile. "Yes."

I ruffled Cinnamon's ears. "They were my family. Still are."

"A werewolf pack that took in a human. Just…because?" he whispered and shook his head. "Who treated her like a wolf, despite her being nothing of the sort."

"She's always been special," Martin said, standing behind me in his human form. He ruffled my hair and smiled down at me.

"Dinner!" Abraham yelled.

"We just ate," Martin chuckled.

"I didn't," I said. "And, I'm starving."

Deryn shifted, and I leapt onto his back again. He ran back to the house and then shifted into human form before linking our fingers and walking into the house.

Dinner was full of laughter and stories from my first encounters. Deryn listened, but he didn't smile much. He didn't look mad, but like he was thinking really hard.

The trip home was quiet, and we stopped at the den to visit Dan. Deryn and Dan went to Dan's office and left me downstairs.

"What's wrong?" Sharla asked, bumping her shoulder against mine.

We both sat on the floor with one twin in each of our laps. Madison was in my lap, curled up in wolf form while I stroked my fingers through her fur.

"Deryn's been acting really weird today. He can't understand why Thor and Martin's pack treats me like they do. I just don't get why it bothers him so much," I admitted.

Sharla shrugged. "When you're used to something being done a certain way, having it done any other way is strange and you won't understand it."

"Yeah, but I just don't get it in this case. So what if they treated me like pack? So what if they still treat me like pack even though I'm in Deryn's now? What does it matter?" I asked.

"Maybe he'll explain it later, once he figures out how to properly explain himself," she suggested.

I hoped so.

"Have you talked to Ezio, since that night?" Sharla asked.

I sighed and shook my head. "No."

"Why not?" she asked.

"It's not on purpose. I just haven't had the time," I explained. "I've been so worried about Nico."

"How is he doing?" she asked.

"Better. He's stressed with all his new duties and the transition," I said. "But, he seems to be doing better now."

"Jolie?" Ezio asked, peeking his head into the living room. He smiled and then saw the pup in my lap, so he squatted down to hug me. "How're you?"

"Good," I said. "How are you? I'm sorry I didn't call you."

He kissed my cheek, then sat back, crossing his legs. "You're busy. I know how it is. Plus, I was fine the next day. The spell was just some type of sleeping spell."

"I can't believe all that happened," I mumbled.

"You're always full of trouble," he teased me. His smile faded a bit, and he leaned forward to smell me. "Where have you been? You smell like a bunch of strange wolves."

"I went and saw my old pack," I explained.

"Martin's pack," Sharla clarified.

"Oh," Ezio said. "How was that?"

"Fun," I said, then glanced at the stairs that led to Dan's office.

"Deryn with Dan?" Ezio asked.

I nodded.

"Talking about you?" he guessed.

I shrugged. "I'm guessing so. Deryn was talking to the pack a lot and then went straight to Dan when we got here."

"Well, I wouldn't worry about it," Ezio said. "I'm sure it's nothing."

I leaned back against the couch and closed my eyes. "I'm so tired," I whispered.

"Just close your eyes and rest," Sharla said. "Ezio and I will stay here and make sure you're safe."

"I can't move anyway," I whispered. "I've got a sleeping pup in my lap. It's against the rules to move now."

Sharla chuckled. "Right you are."

STRONG ARMS PICKED ME UP AGAINST A COMFORTING BODY. "Warm," I whispered.

"I'm sorry I left you for so long," Deryn whispered.

"'s okay."

"Did you have fun today?" he asked.

"Mmhm," I mumbled, eyes still closed.

"What was Ezio doing?" he asked.

"Huh?"

"He was lying on the floor in wolf form near you," he explained.

"Protecting me," I said.

"Protecting you...inside the house?" he asked. I didn't need to see him to know he was smirking and trying not to laugh.

"I'm danger prone," I mumbled, burying my face against his chest.

"You are," he agreed.

He set me down on a big warm bed and I snuggled down into the blankets. He spooned his body around mine and kissed my head. "I love you."

"Love you, too."

"Promise?" he whispered.

I chuckled and snuggled closer to him. "Promise."

CHAPTER 5

JOLIE

I woke to lips kissing their way from my shoulder, to my thigh, and then was pushed onto my back and my clothes removed.

"Morning," I whispered with a chuckle as I opened my eyes, looking down my body to see Deryn sitting with his face above my stomach.

"Morning, beautiful," he whispered. He lowered his head and kissed the bottom of my stomach and then traveled lower.

I gasped as he licked me and within minutes was moaning his name.

He slid inside of me, and I growled with pleasure.

"You're the most beautiful woman in the world," he whispered. "You're a queen, my queen, and I need to make sure you know that."

He pumped his hips, and I arched up to meet him.

"There are lots of people in the house," I reminded him.

He leaned down and whispered, "Then you better be quiet." He kissed me deeply and thrust into me fast and hard.

I bit into his shoulder to hold in my scream as I orgasmed.

"Oh, baby, you're so wet."

"I've been wanting you for a few days," I admitted as I panted with his thrusts.

"You know you just have to ask," he said.

I pushed his chest, and he lay on his back, so I could take control. I sat down slowly and he groaned. "You know how I feel about asking when you're all with me," I said, raising myself up and down slowly, enjoying the feel of him filling me.

He gripped my hips and met my movements with his own. "We need to teach you to communicate telepathically, so you can just ask one of us specifically."

"But, the others would know when we left the room together," I said, throwing my head back as I orgasmed. I tightened around him and couldn't move as much.

"So?" he asked. "It's not like they don't know we have sex?"

"It's different," I growled.

He spun me around, pushing the top half of my body down onto the bed and raising my lower half up until I was on my knees. He slid his hand along my butt, slipping his hand around my hip bone, gripped it, and then thrust into me.

I bit the sheets and screamed into them as he pounded me from behind.

"You're so sexy. You have the most perfect ass I've ever seen," he growled.

He made me orgasm three more times, and then slammed into me one more time, finishing with a loud groan.

We lay in each other's arms for a bit and then took a shower. Dan hugged me when we entered the dining room.

"Morning, Dan," I said as I stepped out of his embrace.

"Morning, Daughter," he said with a wide smile. "Hope you're hungry, because I had a feast put together."

I looked at the empty table and he laughed.

"Not in here, girl. The dining hall," he said and pushed me out

49

of the room. I walked outside, and he led me to one of the many buildings that made up the den. This one was used when they wanted the entire pack to gather together. Dan held open the door for me, and I stepped inside to find all of my exes, my mates, and the other kings. There were a few other people I didn't know as well from each of the four clans, but I was surprised to find them all here.

"What is this?" I asked Dan.

"Business meeting," he said with a smirk.

"This is a trap," I said and folded my arms across my chest. "What do you want?"

"Sit and eat," Dan said, turning away from me to head to the front table where the other kings were.

"Deryn," I growled.

He chuckled. "Well, I was hoping our morning fun might put you in a better and more receptive mood," he said.

"So, you only slept with me to butter me up?" I asked, putting a hand to my heart. I was totally faking it. I knew Deryn and I knew that wasn't why, but it was fun to occasionally mess with my guys.

He pulled me into his arms, dipped me, and kissed me senseless. "You know exactly why I slept with you."

"Because I'm pretty?" I asked.

He chuckled and stood straight, bringing me with him. "Yes."

Nico teleported to me and kissed my cheek. "Hello, gorgeous."

"Hi, Sparkles," I said and kissed his cheek back.

"Ready for fun?" he asked.

"I'm deducting five points from all of you for this deceit," I said.

"Five points?" Nico asked. "That many?"

"Fine, I'll make it ten points," I said and walked by him.

"What are the points for?" Thor asked.

"It's their experience points. They were all really close to leveling up, but now they've lost some points," I said. It was really just a silly thing we said and didn't mean anything.

"Don't I get points for this morning?" Deryn asked.

"No," I said as I took my seat beside Rhys. "You ruined it."

Rhys chuckled and kissed the top of my head. "I warned you guys she wouldn't be receptive if you surprised her with a meeting like this."

"What is this about?" I asked him. "You could be my favorite."

"You don't have a favorite," Deryn scoffed.

"I could," I mumbled and pouted. They all knew I wasn't being serious, though. I could never be so petty.

"Let's eat!" Dan said.

Several wolves from the pack wheeled out carts with trays of food. My mouth watered, and I picked my fork up expectantly. As was usual now, my mates piled food onto my plate and then made their own. I ate most of what they had given me, then leaned back in my chair with a satisfied sigh.

"Most of you know why I've summoned you," Dan said.

I turned and glared at him, but he just smiled at me.

His smile disappeared and he said, "Our spies have obtained information about our enemies."

That didn't narrow it down. I had quite a few enemies now.

"A large contingent of dhampirs have been spotted in a remote area about twenty miles outside of Jinla. They've been seen transporting large crates of weapons and there've been rumors that some local people have been kidnapped by them as well," Dan said.

"Why haven't we destroyed them yet?" Ezio asked.

"Because we don't want to kill the soldier ants until they take us to their hive," Nico said.

That did make sense.

"So, how do we find the hive?" I asked.

"We put a tracking beacon on one of them," Dan said.

I laughed. The sound boomed out of me and grew louder, and I laughed until my stomach hurt.

"What?" Rhys asked.

"We have all this magic and power and you used a piece of technology to track them?" I gasped for breath. "They most likely scan for magic, but I doubt they'd think to scan for pieces of technology."

I could picture Brayden's furious face when he learned how they were tracked.

Speaking of Trident Douche…

"Have there been any sightings of Trident Douche or Bitch-face?" I asked.

There were a few growls around me.

"Not yet," Katar said. "We're searching for them, but have no leads so far."

They were likely hiding, like the rats they were.

"So, why was this meeting orchestrated? Why did you have to trick me into coming?" I asked.

"We have a plan," Dan said. "And—"

"I'm not going to like it," I finished for him. I sighed. "Hit me with it."

"The only way to draw them out is with bait. They won't come out for anything other than their objective," Dan said.

"Me?" I guessed.

"Not you specifically. Your heart," Katar explained.

I glanced at my mates, and then narrowed my eyes at the kings. "No."

"It will work," Dan said.

"You can't guarantee their safety," I growled and stood. "And, that bitch could sever the ties again!"

"We won't let that happen," Deryn assured me.

I spun to face him. "You don't know that! You can't guarantee that! She has that fucking knife and she will cut our ties. Don't you remember how painful it was? Don't you remember how it felt to lose…" I couldn't even finish my sentence. My chest tightened and pain coursed through me. Not true pain, but the memory of the pain. A memory that I could not get rid of.

All four of my mates moved towards me, but I created a shield around myself, keeping them at bay.

"When did she learn that?" Fox asked.

"I will not risk you four. I will not risk any of you. I will not have our bonds severed."

"We're mates. She can't break our bond as mates," Deryn said.

"You were the one who was so adamant about me not removing the curse because of the risk it held. You were the one who held a grudge afterwards," I reminded him, my voice rising and my anger with it. I felt my body heating up and smoke curled from my mouth. "Why are you so quick to risk yourself now? Have you forgotten what it was like?"

"No," Deryn ground out between clenched teeth. "I remember."

"Perhaps you don't remember well enough," I said. My body was glowing as my power rose to the surface. "If you want to risk yourselves, I will have no part in it. I will have no part in this."

"Jolie," Dan said. "Calm down. We aren't—"

"Pain and loss can be forgotten. I understand that. I understand that it dims with time. I knew things were too good to be true. I knew Johann was always partially right."

"Jolie," Nico warned. "Stop."

They didn't remember what it felt like. They didn't remember the horrible gaping hole that had formed with their bonds gone.

"When you've come to your senses, I'll return," I told them.

With a whispered goodbye, I teleported myself away from my mates. I teleported to the other side of the world. And, once I landed, I closed down our bonds as tightly as I could. It hurt, so much that I curled into a ball on the ground. I cried and ugly sobbed as I clutched at my chest. I would not lose them. Not again. Not ever again.

CHAPTER 6

NICO

Jolie had been gone for three days, and we still couldn't locate her. The pain was excruciating and nothing except her being back by my side would fix it.

We had fucked up before, but never this badly. I knew she wouldn't like the idea, but had no idea how upset she would be. I'd tried to explain it to the others, but they were adamant that the plan would work.

Yes, it would work, but Jolie was also right to worry about our bonds. Having our bonds severed had been one of the most painful things I had ever felt, and I couldn't even begin to imagine how it had felt to her, to have four of them cut.

I'd tried every spell I could think of, but still had no luck in finding her.

"This is stupid!" Fox yelled, clutching at his chest.

"We have no one to blame, but ourselves," I whispered.

"She's overreacting," Deryn growled, his fists clenched at his sides as he paced the living room of our house.

"Is she?" I asked, looking at my three brothers. Though we

had no blood relation, they were my brothers through and through.

"What?" Rhys asked, turning away from staring out the window. He'd been staring out the window most of the time, like he thought if he just stared, he would see her coming back.

"She had four bonds cut. Four. Imagine our pain four times over. Then, we bombard her with a meeting like that, to tell her we are going to risk ourselves to draw out the people who have caused her the most pain in the past two years. I think she's reacting pretty appropriately for who she is. I'm more surprised that she didn't destroy anything." The amount of power she had been building, had it been released, would have had catastrophic repercussions.

"She's made her point," Deryn growled. "Why hasn't she come back yet?"

"Are you still planning to use yourself as bait?" I asked Deryn, already knowing the answer. Neither he or Rhys responded. "Then, she hasn't made her point."

"This is—" Rhys began, but I cut him off.

"She doesn't know how else to explain or show us the pain she endured. She is doing what she thinks is the best way to bring us to our senses. What if she volunteered to be used as bait? How would you feel?"

Rhys, Deryn, and Fox all growled.

"Exactly," I whispered, my hand balling into a fist at the thought of her being used as bait.

"Doesn't this mean that she's experiencing this pain four times over as well?" Fox asked, rubbing his chest with the heel of his palm.

I nodded. It was something that worried me the most. She was likely in so much pain, that she might not be able to protect herself.

Rhys's phone rang and he answered it with a grumble. His

entire body went rigid and then he turned on the television in the room to the news station.

"Reports are flooding in of people in Rulan experiencing pain so intense, that they are curled into balls all over, clutching at their chests. Doctors have confirmed that the cause is magical, but have no idea where the source is," the reporter said. They panned to a video showing people lying in the streets of several cities, crying and clutching their chests.

"Fuck," Fox said, turning to me.

I nodded. "She's there."

"Authorities are trying to pinpoint the location of the spell's origin, but have so far been unable to do so," the reporter continued.

"Do you have a spell to shield us from that while we fly closer?" Rhys asked me.

"Yeah," I said breathlessly. She had no idea she was causing others to feel her pain. She would be devastated to learn about it. We had to get to her before someone died.

We all headed to the roof, and Rhys shifted into his dragon form.

I'd wanted to give her more time, but we had to get to her and stop this. We couldn't let people suffer just because we were being stubborn assholes.

CHAPTER 7

JOLIE

I felt them drawing near, but didn't stop them or try to conceal myself. I wasn't certain how they had found me, but I wasn't worried about that.

The pain was so intense, I couldn't move. I had wanted to return yesterday, but hadn't been able to do anything other than sob on the floor. No tears came anymore, my body was dehydrated and my stomach was completely empty.

Deryn tore the door off its hinges and tossed it out into the hallway. He stood there, his eyes blazing, and looked around the room until he found me. Once his eyes landed on me, the fury was gone, replaced by pain and sadness.

Nico rushed in, pushing Deryn aside and dropped to his knees beside me. "Release the bonds," he ordered me.

I opened my mouth, but all that came out was a wail of pain.

"Dammit," Rhys growled.

Nico grabbed me, but as soon as our bodies came into contact, the pain spread to him, and he fell to the floor beside me, his mouth open in a silent scream.

Fox, Rhys, and Deryn dropped to their knees, clutching at their chests.

Fox had tears streaming down his cheeks and he shuffled on his hands and knees closer to me. "Jolie, release the bonds. Do it. Now. You're hurting others. You're projecting your pain and the others in this city are hurting just like you are."

Fuck.

I was so close to blacking out as it was. I didn't have much time left. How had my power spread? How had others been brought into this?

I took a deep breath, and with a mighty heave, released the bonds. Their energy rushed into me and I fainted.

"JOLIE," NICO WHISPERED, HIS LIPS PRESSED LIGHTLY TO MY EAR. "Wake up. Please, love. Please wake up. I can't lose you. I can't lose anyone else."

Hot drops splashed the side of my face. Nico...was crying?

My entire body hurt. Everything felt heavy and strange.

Just opening my eyelids took a huge amount of effort.

Nico's tear-filled eyes met mine and he smiled. "Hello, beautiful."

I'd fucked up. I was only supposed to leave them for a day, make them relive the pain that they'd felt when we had lost our bonds. Or, at least as close to that pain as I could.

"Drink this," Fox ordered me, holding a cup of liquid up to my lips.

Nico helped me sit up, and I drank the strange green juice. It burned as it went down, but once in my stomach, I felt it healing me.

I had no strength to hold myself up, but Nico held me effortlessly.

Nico stroked my hair while Fox stroked his thumb across the hand he held.

My throat wouldn't work yet. I closed my eyes and relaxed at their touches.

"She's awake," Nico said.

"Has she said anything?" Rhys asked.

He sounded like he was across the room. Was he mad at me? Was he avoiding me? I couldn't feel them in the bond, despite it being open.

"No. She's still healing," Fox answered.

"We need to go," Deryn said, his footsteps coming closer.

Nico lifted me in his arms, and I leaned my head on his chest.

"Roof?" Fox asked.

"Yes," Deryn said.

Nico walked to the door, pausing by Deryn as he reached out.

I flinched as his hot hand touched my skin. He jerked his hand back and scowled. "She's so cold."

"Who's there?" a deep voice shouted from somewhere downstairs.

"Go," Rhys said.

All four headed up the stairs and to the roof. Rhys shifted and the three climbed on to his back. Nico set me on Rhys's back, looping an arm around my waist and pulling me back against his chest.

The potion Fox had given me was working, but I didn't have the strength yet to hold onto Rhys. Deryn sat in front of me and I reached up a trembling hand, brushing my fingertips on the edge of the back of his shirt, since that was all I could reach.

He turned and his brow furrowed. He scooted back, closer to me, and said something to Nico, but I couldn't hear. It was only a moment later that my eyes rolled up into the back of my head.

❀

I WOKE STILL IN NICO'S ARMS. HE WAS WALKING, BUT THE ONLY sound I heard was my blood rushing through my body.

He set me down on something soft it felt like a bed and started to move away, but I grabbed his arm, holding him as tightly as I could.

He slid down next to me, wrapping his arms around me.

Warmth from my other side began to fill me. Fox was healing me.

I opened my eyes and met his tear-filled ones.

Slowly, I opened my mouth and said, "How…"

"Shush," Deryn ordered me. "Don't talk yet."

"Sorry," I whispered, tears welling again and spilling over and down my cheeks.

Nico shushed me and kissed my forehead. "Don't apologize," he whispered. "We're the ones who are sorry. We're jerks and we are sorry."

"I'm sorry," Deryn whispered his lips next to my ear and his cheek against mine. "I'm sorry."

Maybe it hadn't been for nothing? Maybe, they understood what I'd been trying to say.

"I'm an ass and I'm so sorry. I always screw shit up with you," Deryn whispered. "I shouldn't have tricked you like that. I shouldn't have agreed to that plan. I knew you wouldn't like it, and yet I went along with it anyway. I'm not fit to be your mate."

I grabbed his arm, squeezing as hard as I could. He rubbed his face against mine and I felt the dampness from his cheek.

"Someday, I'll learn to actually look at things from your point of view. I'll try to get better. I'll try to think things through before acting. I can't lose you. And, I know you can't lose us either. We won't be using ourselves as bait. Okay? We promise," Deryn whispered, sniffling.

Nico moved away from me, his body replaced by a warmer one as Rhys lay beside me. He slid his hand along my cheek and rubbed his thumb over my cheekbone. "We're sorry, baby. We're so sorry."

"I shouldn't have run off," I managed to say, new tears streaming down my face. "I'm sorry," I sobbed.

When would I learn to stop acting without thinking? When would I learn to stop being so damn childish?

"Shush," Rhys ordered me. "Just lay and heal."

"Did you eat at all?" Deryn asked.

"No," I whispered, sniffling. "No food or drink."

Just pain. Lots and lots of pain.

"Drink this," Deryn ordered me.

I opened my eyes and let Rhys sit me up before drinking from the offered cup.

This cup held a potion that helped restore magic reserves and healed the body faster than others. It also tasted like shit.

I swallowed it, and then coughed a few moments.

Rhys kissed my temple as he held me up. "I'm sorry."

"I'm sorry," Deryn said.

"I'm sorry, too," Fox said.

"Me, too," Nico said.

"We won't use ourselves as bait," Fox said.

"Promise?" I asked as I looked at each of them.

They all nodded.

"We promise," they all said.

"I'm sorry," I said and started crying again, wrapping my arms around Rhys's neck, and then hugged Deryn. Fox leaned forward across my body to hug me and let Nico do the same.

"No more talking," Deryn said.

Rhys lay me back down and then spooned his body around mine. "Sleep, Jolie."

Deryn spooned his body on my other side and before I could ask where Nico and Fox were going, Nico used a spell to put me to sleep.

When I woke, I sat on the edge of the bed, staring down at my hands.

"What's up?" Deryn asked groggily, wiping at his eyes as he sat up beside me.

"I'm sorry," I whispered.

He pulled me onto his lap and wrapped me up in his arms. "We all get a little carried away from time to time."

"I can't lose you," I whispered, tears streaming down my face.

His hold tightened, and he kissed the top of my head. "You won't."

Rhys sat up, his eyes still closed as he pulled me from Deryn's lap, and into his. Deryn held one of my hands, and I took several deep breaths to relax.

"We need to find them, but there has to be another way," I said.

"We'll think of something," Rhys replied in his grumbling sleepy voice, eyes still closed. He was so not a morning person.

"They'll slip up eventually," Deryn said. "The bad guys always do."

"What day is it? Don't you guys have work?" I asked, trying to look around Rhys for the clock on the bedside table.

"It's Saturday," Deryn answered.

"Shoot, I have to go to see the elves today," I said, jumping from Rhys's lap. My legs wobbled a moment, but they held me up. After a quick shower, I felt back to my old self.

Fox was the only one left in the room when I finished changing. I'd been instructed to dress fancy, so I put on a red backless dress I had recently purchased. It was a little snug in the stomach, but not uncomfortably.

"What's up, buttercup?" I asked with a smile.

He held out his hand, a scowl on his face.

Serious Fox was never a good sign.

I went to him, set my hand in his, and let him pull me down to sit in his lap.

He nuzzled me behind my ear and whispered, "Promise me something?"

"Hm?" I asked, my pulse hammering at his deep and quiet tone.

"If you want to leave, if you want some space, at least take me with you. Let me be nearby so if something happens, I can get to you. You could have died. I don't know what I would do if you died. Probably destroy something."

The thought of Fox destroying something was almost funny. Yes, he was strong and powerful, but he was so often relaxed and non-aggressive, it was easy to forget.

"I'm sorry," I whispered, nuzzling his neck and placing a gentle kiss on it.

"Don't apologize. Just, promise me?"

"I promise," I whispered, wrapping my arms around his neck and squeezing.

"You're my world, Jolie. We screwed up. We did forget how painful it had been. We did forget what it was like to lose you. I don't want to condone your tactic, but it worked. We all remembered what it was like, how awful it was. I don't want to be separated from you again. Never again."

Hearing him admit that what I had done had worked made the guilt lessen. Not that I liked hurting them, but I was glad that what I had done had succeeded.

"Never again," I agreed, squeezing him.

He stood, supporting my weight with one arm beneath my butt, while I kept my arms around his neck. "Now that we got that serious business out of the way, let's go have fun!"

"What are we doing today?" I asked.

"Elven fun!" he said.

I looked up at him, and he just smiled brightly, radiating happiness and warmth.

"Whatever you want to do," I said, resting my head on his chest as he carried me.

"Whatever I want, huh? Well, in that case we aren't leaving the house for a week," he said in a rumbling whisper in my ear.

"Naughty elf," I quipped.

He chuckled. "Dad will kill me if I don't bring you home. Mother has been demanding to see you, too. She's got something up her sleeve and I'm not sure what it is. It's worrisome."

"Your parents love me," I reminded him. "I'm sure it is fine."

"I think they like you better than me," he said with a pout.

I bit the sensuous lip he had stuck out, and he growled, his hold tightening.

"Tease," he grumbled when I released his lip.

"Not a tease a promise for later," I replied.

"We don't have to stay long, right? We could pop in, give greetings, then come back home, right?" he said.

"You can wait," I said, jumping from his arms as we got to the garage.

"I *can*, but that doesn't mean I want to," he replied, unlocking his car.

I climbed in and buckled up. They'd only recently stopped using drivers for everything. Dan had argued with Deryn for hours about us needing to use a driver, but we'd won out in the end. We still used drivers for some things, but for the most part the guys drove now.

"When did you learn to teleport?" Fox asked as he started the car.

I shrugged. "A while ago."

"And why didn't you tell us?"

"Because I figured it might come in handy at some point," I replied. And, I had been right.

"What else do you know how to do?" he asked, backing out of the garage.

"Well, I did learn this new thing with my tongue, and—"

He groaned and then laughed. "You're such a brat."

"You love me," I said with a wide smile.

He shifted into first and headed away from the house. "That I do, my love. That I do."

"So, what does elven fun consist of?" I asked.

"A party," he said.

"For?"

"Uh, for a special event," he said, skirting around a proper answer.

"Fox," I said in a growl.

"Dad's birthday," he said.

"What! I don't have a gift for him. We have to stop somewhere first and—"

Fox shook his head, stopping me. "We have a gift. I got one that is from both of us."

"What is it?" I asked.

"Well, I can't tell you yet. We have to talk to my mom first," he said, his brows furrowing and his grip tightening on the steering wheel.

Was that fear?

"What is it, Fox? Why are you scared?"

"It's probably nothing. I'm just being paranoid," he said.

"Fox," I moaned and leaned against the door. "You're doing that thing again."

"I know!" he said and sighed. "Look, I can't say anything until we see Mom. Okay? The others will be there, too."

"The others?" I asked.

"You know, your other mates," he teased. "Or am I just so handsome that you forgot about them?"

I chuckled and leaned over to kiss his cheek. "You are very handsome."

"Deryn still has the best butt, though. That irritates me," he grumbled.

I burst into a fit of laughter. I couldn't help myself. I laughed so hard that I clutched at my hurting stomach.

"Laugh it up," he grumbled.

"Kit, you have an amazing ass, too. I don't understand these complexes you boys have. You're all fucking gorgeous and could get any girl you wanted."

"There's only one girl I want," he said. "And she keeps staring at Deryn's ass as he walks by."

I bit my lip to keep from laughing again. "I look at yours when you walk by, too."

"Not the same," he grumbled.

"You also lose all self-control when Rhys has his shirt off."

Well, in my defense, Rhys had a perfect chest.

"Are you feeling self-conscious?" I asked, leaning over to rest my head on his shoulder.

"What about me is better than them?" he asked.

"Well…" I blushed and turned away from him.

"Well?" he asked.

"You are the biggest," I said.

His eyebrows rose and then he laughed. "I am."

"You already knew that," I said.

He shrugged. "It happens. When you know guys for your entire life, at some point you see their junk."

"So, there you go," I said.

"So, I just need to walk around airing my junk out to get you to look at me?" he asked.

I burst into another fit of laughter. "Please, don't," I begged.

He smirked. "Oh, alright. I'll keep it contained until it's needed."

"You're the sexiest elf I know," I told him. "If that counts for anything."

He smiled, a purely dazzling, happy smile. "That does. Thanks."

"You're welcome."

CHAPTER 8

RHYS

"Still having issues?" Dad asked as he entered.

I lay on my back in the gym, sweat dripping from my body, and my breathing coming in great, heaving pants.

"Yes," I admitted with a groan.

He sat down beside me, staring at the wall of the gym, but really just looking off into space while he thought.

I waited patiently, knowing he was thinking and needed a moment to get his thoughts in order.

"Have you told Jolie?" he asked, glancing down at me.

I winced. "No. I was going to the other day, but then the shit hit the fan and—"

"Did you apologize to her?" he asked.

I sat up and glared at him. "You were in on the plan, too," I reminded him.

"I was against it, but willing to do what the majority voted," he said. "I told you Jolie wouldn't go for it."

I sighed and rubbed a hand down my face. "I don't think I've screwed up so badly before," I told him. "She was right. We had forgotten how painful it was."

"I hadn't," he said. "You were utterly destroyed when your bond was cut. I should have recorded it so you could rewatch the absolute terror and pain on your face when it happened."

"I'll tell her soon," I promised, wanting to change the subject and not think about the time I had almost lost Jolie.

"Have you tried with her near you?" he asked, looking at my chest. "Perhaps you're holding back with her being away from you."

He could have a point, but—

"It wasn't an issue before I met her," I reminded him.

He shrugged. "Everything changes when you find your queen and mate," he said. "You should bring her here and try with her in the room."

It wasn't a bad idea.

"Okay," I agreed.

He glanced at the clock on the wall. "You should go shower and get ready. You're going to Katar's party, right?"

I nodded and then winced. Yet another surprise waiting for Jolie. Or, well, potential surprise.

"What's wrong?" Dad asked.

"Nothing," I said and sighed at his raised eyebrow. "Possibly nothing. I don't know. We'll see."

He chuckled and ruffled my hair like he used to when I was a boy. "You're always up to something, son. That hasn't changed." He stood and held out his hand. I accepted and let him pull me to my feet. "If you need anything, I'm always here."

I nodded. "I know. Thanks."

He started walking away, and I called out, "Dad?"

He turned to face me.

"What do you do when you screw up with Mom?"

Dad smiled. "I buy her gifts and remind her that she's my

queen. The one goddess I worship, and that I'm an idiot for risking that."

I nodded.

"She loves you. She has sacrificed herself for you many times. Perhaps it is time for you to take over that role," he said and waved as he left the room.

My beautiful, infuriating mate was constantly throwing herself in danger. She wanted to protect us, I knew that, but just like she didn't want to lose us, we didn't want to lose her. We were in the beginnings of a war, and I had no idea what to expect. I wanted to protect her and to do that, I needed to be at my peak.

But, for quite a while now, I had been having issues with my scales. My scales used to automatically cover a part of my body that was in danger, but since that day I was shot, they hadn't been doing that. They hadn't been doing anything automatically, and I had no idea why.

With a sigh, I headed to the shower. Time to face our next ordeal.

CHAPTER 9

JOLIE

There were quite a few cars parked in front of Katar and Kara's house, and I could hear music playing.

Fox opened my door, and held out his hand. I let him help me from the car and smoothed down the dress I wore.

"You're gorgeous," he told me and kissed me deeply. "I love you."

"I love you, too," I said, smiling at him.

Fox lead me into the house, despite the party obviously going on in the backyard. I opened my mouth to ask what we were doing inside, when I saw my other mates waiting in the living room with Kara.

"What's going on?" I asked, planting my feet and coming to a halt in the hallway. This looked like an intervention. What the hell could I need an intervention for? I didn't smoke or do drugs. I enjoyed sweets, but so did all of my mates. I hadn't even been playing much videogames, so it couldn't be about that.

"Easy," Fox said, running a hand down my arm. "This isn't an intervention or anything."

He tried to pull me forward, but I yanked my hand away. "What's going on?" I asked again.

Kara walked to me, a smile on her face. She opened her arms, and I stepped forward to hug her. She smelled like flowers and gave motherly hugs that made you want to relax and tell her all the things going on in your life.

"The boys are worried about your health, so they asked me to check you out," she whispered into my ear. "They're being good mates, so please don't fight me on this."

I sighed and rested my head on her shoulder. "Okay, but I feel fine."

She pushed me back at arm's length and smiled. "Then this should be quick!"

Her eyes began to glow, and then she ran her hand from my head to my feet, and then back up again. She released the power, her eyes returning to normal as she smiled warmly at me. "Jolie, I need you to sit down."

Oh, no. That wasn't good.

Rhys brought me a chair, smiling at me with tears pooling in his eyes.

What was going on?

"Am I dying?" I asked softly.

My mates tensed and all eyes locked on me.

Kara chuckled softly. "No, darling daughter. You are not dying."

I sat in the chair and folded my arms across my chest. "Then, why am I being told to sit and why is Rhys trying not to cry?"

"I've got something in my eye," he lied, rubbing at his face.

Kara knelt in front of me and took my hands in hers. "You are pregnant, Jolie."

The world stopped, all sound disappeared, and I felt faint. This was why she had me sit down.

Pregnant? No. I'd been taking contraceptives. I had been

careful to take them and never missed a day. My period was supposed to start in a day or two, so I wasn't technically late.

"You're sure?" I asked.

Kara nodded, smiling wider. "Yes. You are one hundred percent pregnant."

"Do you know whose it is?" I asked.

I saw my mates scowl out of the corner of my eye, but didn't turn to face them.

"No. We won't know for a few weeks," she said.

"Dammit," I whispered. Hot tears slid down my cheeks, and I sniffled. This wasn't supposed to happen yet. It wasn't the right time!

My four mates rushed to me, dropping to their knees and putting one hand each on me.

"What is it?" Fox asked. "Why are you upset? Why are you sad?"

"I thought you wanted children?" Rhys asked.

"I didn't want to have a child before we caught Brayden and Justina," I sobbed. "I didn't want to put yet another person in danger. It's hard enough keeping you four safe and now I have a baby to deal with. How am I going to protect the baby? What if she kills the baby?"

"We won't let her get to you. She can't harm our baby if she can't get to you," Deryn said, squeezing my leg. "We will protect you and our baby," he swore.

"Our baby is our top priority now," Rhys said with a nod. "We won't let anything happen to risk his or her life."

"No one's touching you," Fox growled, his eyes glowing.

"We will do everything we need to keep you both safe," Nico said. He rested his hand on my stomach and smiled, his eyes lighting with joy. "We're having a baby. This is a time to be happy."

"You keep saying 'our baby,' but you don't know whose it is," I said, wiping at my eyes.

"It doesn't matter who the technical father is," Rhys said. "We're all your mates and the baby will be all of ours."

"Just like the baby will be my grandchild, no matter who the father is," Kara said, wiping my cheeks with a soft cloth. "You and your baby are a treasure. You will be protected, and nothing will happen to you two. I will be your personal midwife, if you need it."

Rhys, Fox, and Deryn placed their hands on my stomach, and I felt a small magical spark zip between them and my stomach.

I was pregnant.

"We're having a baby," I whispered, tears returning to my eyes, but for a whole new reason. I had been worried I wouldn't be able to have a child, since sirens were almost infertile.

I stood, four sets of arms surrounded me, and each took turns kissing my cheek.

"What's going on?" Katar asked, worry evident in his tone.

The guys stepped away from me, except for Fox, who stood at my side with a proud smile.

"Happy birthday," he said to Katar.

"Thank you," Katar said, his eyes not leaving mine. "But, I'd like to know what's going on with my daughter."

I smiled at him and walked a step closer. "You're going to be a grandfather," I said.

His eyes widened and he looked at my stomach...then Kara, who nodded...and then back to me. "You're pregnant?"

I nodded, smiling wider.

He smiled, picked me up, and spun around in a circle while he cheered. "I'm going to be a grandpa!"

I chuckled and patted him on the shoulder.

He set me down and then reached towards my stomach, but stopped a few inches away, and looked at me. "May I?"

I nodded.

He set his hand on my stomach and tears sprang to his eyes. "A child. I can't wait to see it."

"Well, you'll have to wait nine months," I said and chuckled.

He looked up at me with furrowed brows. "What?"

"Nine months. That's a human gest—"

"You're not human," Nico reminded me.

"What?" I asked, turning to face him. I knew I wasn't human, but I didn't know that mattered.

"Our gestation periods aren't like humans," Rhys said. "They're faster."

"It's to make it easier to stay safe," Kara explained.

"How long?" I asked.

"Six months," Nico answered. "That's what the research I did on sirens said."

Six months! That was so soon.

"Easy," Deryn whispered, wrapping an arm around my waist, and pulling me against his side. "We've got plenty of time. It's six months still, that's half a year."

"I need to tell my dad," I whispered.

"How will you communicate with him?" Kara asked.

"I'll have to send a messenger to Atlantis," I said.

"Can we tell our dads?" Deryn asked.

"They're coming tonight, aren't they?" Katar asked.

Deryn and Rhys nodded.

I looked over at Nico, the only one who didn't have a father to tell, but he just smiled at me.

"Why don't we bring them in and tell them when they get here?" Katar suggested. "Then we can all celebrate together."

"I ruined your party," I realized and felt awful.

He shook his head and laughed. "Ruined it? This is the best present I have ever received!" He looked at my stomach again and said, "I'm going to spoil the shit out of this kid."

I laughed and tears sprang to my eyes.

"What's going on?" Dan asked from the entryway.

"Back here!" Katar called.

Deryn's grip on my waist tightened a moment, and then he relaxed.

"The host is missing from his own party," Dan said, smiling broadly as he clapped Katar on the back. "Happy birthday, old friend."

"Thank you, Dan," Katar replied.

"Where's Emrys?" Katar asked.

"Outside," Dan answered.

"I'll get him," Rhys said, and quickly left the room.

Dan looked at me and Deryn. "What's going on?"

Katar patted his shoulder. "All in good time, friend. Just wait until Emrys is here."

Emrys and Rhys came in, and Emrys paused by Dan, but frowned at me. "What's going on?"

"Jolie has some news," Katar said, beaming.

"You're all going to be grandfathers," I said, smiling.

Emrys's eyes widened, and he glanced at Rhys.

Dan whooped loudly, and picked me up in a bone crunching hug. "Woohoo!" he yelled as he held me. He set me down, and I realized I had never seen him smile so wide before. "This is the best news, ever!"

"Congratulations," Emrys said, pulling me into a hug. "I can't wait to meet your child."

Was he worried it wouldn't be Rhys's? Why had he looked at Rhys when I told them?

"You're frowning," Emrys said. "Why?"

"I thought you'd be more excited," I said, which was partially true.

"I am very excited," he said, smiling. "I'm just not as rambunctious as some." He glanced at Dan and then focused on me again.

"We'll be able to tell who the father is in a few weeks," I said softly.

His smile wilted. "Okay."

Rhys came up behind me and wrapped his arms around me, resting both hands on my stomach. He dropped his head so his lips were right by my ear. "He doesn't care who the father is, baby."

"Why did he look at you like that, then?" I asked.

"Because I knew something was up, but hadn't thought it would be this," Emrys said. He smiled and rested a hand on my shoulder. "It doesn't matter who fathered the child. It's your child, and therefore it is my grandchild. That's all there is to it. Okay?"

I nodded quickly, trying to stop the tears threatening to spill over. It didn't make sense to me, but I was incredibly grateful.

"Come on! Let's go celebrate!" Katar said, tossing an arm around my shoulders and pulling me away from Rhys. "It's my birthday and I'm going to be a grandfather! I have two reasons to celebrate."

"No alcohol," Fox called after me.

I scowled and groaned. "Oh, dammit!"

Everyone laughed, but me.

"I'll get you a virgin daiquiri," Katar promised. "It will taste just as good."

"Alright," I pouted, but then smiled up at him and kissed his cheek. "Thank you."

"For?" he asked, and pushed open the back door.

There had to be over two hundred people. Some were dancing, most were drinking, and some were obviously drunk already.

"For being excited about this baby," I said. "I'm honestly still not sure I've wrapped my head around it yet."

"You realize that your mates are going to be even more protective, right?" he asked, leaning close so no one else would hear us.

I sighed. "Yeah. They're going to try to wrap me in bubble wrap."

"You'd just pop all the bubbles and make the wrap pointless,"

Katar teased.

I laughed. "Too true."

"Jolie, you can't put yourself in danger anymore. I know you want to keep your mates safe, but your job now is to keep your baby safe, which means you stay safe. So, no more heroics. Let your mates be the heroes. That's their job."

"I know," I whispered. "I just don't want to lose them."

"Losing you will devastate them. Losing you *and* your child will destroy them. I can't let that happen. If need be, I'll give you guards," Katar said.

We made our way through the people, and Katar smiled and talked to those he passed by.

"I'll be on my best behavior," I promised.

He chuckled. "That's not very reassuring."

We came to a stop at a temporary bar, where a woman was mixing drinks.

"Virgin daiquiri," Katar ordered for me.

"Right away, sir," she said, and poured what she'd mixed into a glass before handing it to a nearby person, and then starting on my drink.

"Stop stealing her from me," Dan growled, as he weaved through people and pulled me from Katar to drape an arm around my shoulders and pull me to his side.

"You see her more often than I do," Katar countered.

Deryn spun me away from Dan, snagging the drink the bartender held out as he did. "I'm stealing my mate back," he told them.

I laughed and took my drink from him. "Hello, handsome."

He kissed my cheek. "Hey, beautiful." He led me a little way away from the crowd, sliding his arm around my waist as we walked.

I took a drink and sighed happily. It was so good. "What are we doing over here?" I asked.

"We just wanted to get you a bit away from the crowd," Rhys

said, coming to stand on my other side.

Nico slid his hands around my waist from behind and kissed the back of my neck. "Plus, you keep getting stolen from us."

I leaned back against him and turned my head to kiss his cheek. "You act like you like me, or something," I teased.

"Just a little bit," he whispered in my ear, resting his hands on my stomach.

"Everyone," Katar called.

The music stopped and everyone quieted.

"Thank you for coming to celebrate my birthday," Katar said, looking out over the crowd. "You've all made this one special day." His eyes settled on me and his smile widened. "So, let's enjoy the night with drinks and food!"

Everyone clapped and a dozen people came out of the main house, carrying trays of food.

"Food," I whispered, my stomach grumbling in agreement.

All four of my mates chuckled.

"I'll get her food," Fox said, kissing my cheek as he walked by.

"There are some seats over here," Deryn said, pointing to tables that had been set up.

I was incredibly unobservant tonight. I hadn't seen any of them.

"What's wrong?" Nico asked, coming to walk on my side as we headed to the tables.

"Just realizing I'm unobservant tonight," I admitted.

"You've got a lot on your mind," he said, linking our fingers together.

I leaned my shoulder against his as we walked. "Everything is going to be alright, isn't it?"

He squeezed my hand and smiled. "Yes, my queen. Everything is going to be just fine."

Fox brought me a huge plate of food and then sat with me while the others went to make their plates.

I sat with the four most important men in my life, eating at a birthday party for one of my fathers-in-law, and silently stressed. A baby was a huge change. We wouldn't be able to go out whenever we wanted. We wouldn't have free time. I would have a tiny being who depended on me to survive. Our lives would be focused on keeping this new being alive and healthy.

Fox set his hand on my leg while talking to the others. It did nothing to ease my worry.

I hadn't planned to have a child yet. Yes, I wanted a child, but not until we were safe. Though, if I were honest with myself, we were never safe. There were always random threats and there would always be evil in the world.

We had so much work to do to baby-proof the house. There were so many things we needed to buy. I didn't even know what dragon, wolf, mage, or elf babies were like. Did we run the risk of a dragon baby burning down the nursery?

Nursery. We needed to convert one of the rooms into a nursery.

"Jolie," Deryn whispered in my ear, his chin coming to rest on my shoulder. "What's wrong?"

"There's so much to do before the baby comes," I whispered.

He wrapped his arms around me. "We have plenty of time. We can figure out all the things we need to do tomorrow, and make a game plan. Okay?"

"I'm just not prepared," I whispered, closing my eyes. "I wasn't expecting this yet."

"None of us were," he reminded me. "But, we have each other, and we will get through it together."

He was right, but that didn't stop me from worrying.

"Have some cake," Rhys said, sliding a big slice of white cake with chocolate frosting on the table in front of me.

"Cake!" I gasped, leaning away from Deryn to grab a fork.

Deryn was right. We had each other. We could make a plan and get everything in order in the next six months.

I hoped.

CHAPTER 10

DERYN

Jolie was pregnant. I stared at the wall of my bedroom, letting it sink in fully. Last night, when we had confirmed it, I'd wanted to steal her away and hide her from everyone.

My little siren was so danger prone, and I could not bear the thought of her or our child being injured.

I felt bad for wishing the child was mine, but I knew the others felt the same. We all wanted the child to be sired by us, but we would still love and raise the child as our own, even if it wasn't truly ours. What mattered, was that it was Jolie's.

I had wanted to cry in joy, knowing that she was pregnant. We had all been worried she wouldn't be fertile enough to conceive, but that was obviously not the case.

"Hey," Rhys said from my doorway.

"What's up?" I asked, turning to face him.

"What are you thinking about?" he asked.

"The baby," I admitted.

He smiled, no, beamed. Rhys rarely beamed like that. "It's pretty awesome, right?"

I nodded. "I can't wait to see what the baby looks like."

"I know most dads want sons, but I would love to have a miniature Jolie running around," he said.

I felt the same.

"We're about to head out for the shopping trip," he said. "That's why I came to get you."

"Oh, right."

Jolie had decided she wanted to go to a baby store to look at furniture and begin decorating the nursery. We knew it would help ease her stress, or hoped it would, so we all agreed to go with her.

I followed Rhys down to the garage, where everyone was already inside one of our SUVs. Dad had ordered us to keep a guard and driver at all times, now that Jolie was pregnant. I knew he was just as excited as we were.

"Morning," I greeted Ezio.

Ezio nodded, but his eyes were focused on Jolie, who was fumbling with a pad of paper in her lap in the front passenger seat. Normally, I would have been jealous or angry at his attention on her, but for once, I was glad to have him. Ezio loved Jolie, and he would sacrifice himself in an instant for her. When I had told him Jolie was pregnant, he'd become even more protective. He hovered near her, ready to catch her if she tripped or fainted. Part of me knew that I should be the one hovering, but I also knew Jolie would hate to have us fawning over her so closely. She liked to be independent and strong, which she was, but for some reason, Ezio fawning over her didn't make her upset. Perhaps it was her knowledge that he wasn't her mate, so he was just being a doting friend? I wasn't certain. But, I could endure his presence, knowing it meant she would be safer.

"Buckle up," Ezio ordered Jolie.

She complied without even an eye roll.

She would have growled had I ordered her.

What was it about her exes that made her more compliant? Was she just more likely to rebel when it was a true authority figure, like her alpha or her mates? That had to be it.

"Do you have your list?" I asked her.

Fox rolled his eyes at me, and Nico snickered softly.

"Right here!" she announced happily, waving the pad of paper. She'd become obsessed with lists lately.

"Alright, then let's go!" I said, smiling at her and sending all the love I felt for the beautiful woman in the front seat down our bond.

She still hadn't figured out how to communicate telepathically through the bond yet. Fox and Nico had tried to work with her on it, but she just became frustrated and angry. So, we decided to set that task aside until she wasn't so stressed out.

"*She quit,*" Nico said through our warrior bond, his head tilted so I could see his face.

My entire body tensed. "*What?*" I asked, turning to face him fully.

"*She sent in her resignation this morning,*" he explained. "*She told me that she was too stressed with the baby to even think about work and since we had all told her before she could quit and we would provide for her, she did it.*"

Wow. I never thought she would quit her job. She loved it. That's why we hadn't pushed her too much, because we could tell she truly loved her work.

"I should be happy," I whispered out loud to him, "but this just makes me worry even more."

He nodded. "Same."

CHAPTER 11

JOLIE

The store I had chosen was three stories tall and had everything I would need for the baby. My mates hung back together, whispering to each other. Normally, I would have been irritated, but I had more important things on my mind.

"Ezio, can you get a shopping cart?" I asked. Ezio had been hovering over me ever since Dan had assigned him to me.

I had expected Deryn to growl at Ezio by now, but he hadn't so much as twitched his lip.

I glanced over at my mates.

They all smiled at me.

Suspicious.

I had known they would be happy once I was pregnant, but I'd underestimated how happy they would be. I had also underestimated the kings' reactions. Katar had warned me my mates would be overprotective, but the kings were much worse. Dan had tried to convince me to move into his house at the wolf den, stating it would be safer than our house. I had politely declined, and he had assigned Ezio to guard me.

Ezio returned with a cart. "Do you want to push it, so you can lean on it?" he asked, his brows narrowed.

I chuckled and patted his arm. "I'm barely pregnant, Ezio. I don't need help walking."

"I could carry you," he offered.

I put my hands on my hips. "You will do no such thing! I am perfectly capable of walking."

Fox slid his arm around my waist, and pulled me into his side. "I'll keep an arm around her," he said.

Ezio nodded in approval, and we started down the first aisle of the store.

The first stop was bottles. I stared at the wall of bottles. There were dozens of different shapes and sizes, and so many different nipple options that I didn't know where to begin. Some were marketed for werewolves and others for dragons. Maybe I should have waited until we found out who the sire was before choosing?

"Just get one of each," Fox suggested. "We can see what works and get more of that winning item."

I smiled and kissed his cheek. "Good idea."

Rhys leapt up to grab a bottle off the third shelf, and Deryn jumped up to grab one from the second shelf, tossing them into the cart Ezio was still standing behind.

"You could just ask for help," a store attendant said with a chuckle.

I turned and the older woman smiled at me. "First child?" she guessed.

I nodded.

"Who's the father?" she asked.

I glanced at my mates and bit my lip. "Um…"

"We are," All four said at the same time.

Her eyes widened. "Well, that doesn't really narrow down the specifics, but I suppose it is better to plan for every possibility. If you give me your list, I can help you find the items you need."

"Thanks, but I would prefer to look on my own," I told her, clutching my list a bit tighter.

"Nonsense, the Princess of the Four Clans of Jinla shouldn't have to do the shopping herself," she said, stepping closer to me with her hand out.

Ezio shot between us, his teeth bared. "She said, 'no thank you.' So, please leave her alone."

The woman had immediately taken several steps back, her eyes wide. "Yes, sir," she said and disappeared off into the store.

"Ezio," I said with a sigh.

"Sorry," he mumbled, dropping his head and going back to the cart.

"We'll get the rest of the bottles," Fox said, giving my side a squeeze.

I kissed his cheek and walked to Ezio, bumping my hip into his. "Hey. Talk to me."

He sighed. "I'm sorry. I just hate it when people can't take a hint. Or, straight answers. You clearly stated you didn't want her help. I don't want you getting stressed out or worked up. It could negatively impact the baby."

I hugged him, and he rested his chin on top of my head with a sigh. "Ezio, you are not responsible for me and the baby. Yes, we appreciate you being here to help keep me safe, but you don't need to stress yourself out trying to keep me from being stressed. You being stressed is going to stress me out. Understand?"

He growled and grumbled something that sounded like agreement, so I patted his back and continued on the shopping trip.

After three hours, I finally conceded defeat, leaning heavily against Fox as Deryn and Rhys paid for the shopping cart full of items we had gathered to purchase.

"What do you want to do now?" Fox asked, and rubbed his hand up and down my left arm.

"I think it's time to take you guys bulk food shopping," I said.

"More shopping?" Nico asked.

"We should eat first," I advised. "That way we aren't hungry while we're there."

"Plus, you need food," Ezio said, holding out a water bottle.

I drank it without argument and nodded. "I am hungry."

"Where would you like to eat?" Fox asked.

"Anywhere is fine," I said.

"Let's eat somewhere that's quick, so we can do our shopping, and then get her home," Nico suggested.

Fox nodded in agreement.

"Ready?" Deryn asked from the register. The cart was now full of shopping bags.

"Ready," I called back, heading towards them.

"We're going to get some quick food, and then Jolie wants to take us to another shopping place," Fox explained.

"This shopping trip wasn't enough for you?" Rhys teased.

I stuck my tongue out at him, ignoring his taunting.

They packed our purchases into the back, then went through a drive-through, purchasing ten bags of food. I scarfed down three burgers and a large fry before we reached the grocery store I had directed Ezio to.

"This looks like a regular grocery store," Deryn said.

"It's their bulk aisle that we're interested in today," I explained.

"I thought you were going to take us to that store where you can buy a hundred rolls of toilet paper at once," Nico said.

I chuckled. "No, that will have to be a different day. I don't have the energy for that store."

We all climbed out, and Deryn grabbed a shopping cart, standing on it and using one foot to propel it faster down the aisles.

"To the left, and then it will be the back right corner," I directed Deryn.

He nodded, sliding the cart around the corner without tipping it over.

"He's such a child," Fox said with a sigh.

I laughed. "You're one to talk."

He opened his mouth in mock shock. "Me?"

I kissed his cheek. "Your childlike joy is part of what I love about you."

He smirked, but said nothing.

Deryn did a small circle and then pushed his cart forward again, giving me a perfect view of his ass.

"Stop staring at his butt," Fox grumbled.

I snickered. "Well, it's there for my viewing. I can't help it."

"I need to do more squats," Fox mumbled.

Nico laughed and patted Fox's shoulder. "Just accept that Deryn's got the nicest butt out of all of us."

"No," Fox said. "I refuse to lose."

"What are you losing?" Ezio asked.

"Nicest ass," Fox replied.

Ezio threw back his head and laughed, the sound echoing off the tall shelves of the store.

We finally made it to the bulk food section and I smiled at my gathered guys. "Here. You take these bags." I tore a bag from the roll. "And, you fill it up with food from one of the bins."

"What do the bins hold?" Rhys asked, peering over at them.

"Spices, pasta shells, trail mix, chocolate, and more," I explained.

They looked at the bins with wide eyes.

"So, go ahead and get whatever you want," I said, heading towards the first bin where I could see malt chocolate balls.

"We just fill up the bags with as much of whatever item we want?" Fox asked.

I nodded. "And they charge you by weight."

Rhys started down the aisles, looking at each item. Deryn tore off five bags, and began spooning out various things into them.

"Make sure you label them with the item number from the bins," I called out before I forgot.

"Candy!" Fox called from the other side of the bins I was on.

I chuckled.

"Your mates are very easily entertained," Ezio said.

"They don't get out to experience human establishments often. The first time they went to a grocery store was a year ago when I had the flu."

"That must have been one strange trip," Ezio said. "I don't think Deryn has ever been around a sick human before."

"They thought I was dying," I said with a smirk.

He laughed. "I can imagine."

"Clearly you've been around humans more often than them," I commented. Truthfully, I knew very little about what had happened to Ezio between us breaking up and seeing him at the Summit.

He nodded. "I dated a couple humans, so I have a little experience with them."

"Someday, I'd like to hear your story," I told him, scooping some malt balls into my bag.

"Okay," he agreed.

"These bags aren't big enough," Rhys complained.

"Can we just take the entire barrel?" Deryn asked.

I laughed and shook my head. "No, just use the small bags. If you want to get a huge amount, we can order it. This was just supposed to be an adventure into the lives of humans for you. We don't buy huge bulks like you do, since we eat a lot less. One of these bags filled with taco seasoning lasted me over a year."

"A year?" Nico asked, scowling at the bag in his hand. "That's a long time."

"Well, I only made one pound of meat at a time, since I only ate a couple tacos each night," I admitted.

"Now you eat at least a pound of beef each night," Fox said. I still couldn't see him, since he was on the next aisle, but I could hear him just fine.

"And I suppose I'll be eating even more now?" I asked.

Ezio, Nico, Rhys, and Deryn all nodded their heads in response.

"You should pick out some treats," Nico said. "So we can keep them on hand when you get a craving."

That wasn't a bad idea. "Okay," I said, grabbing more bags and beginning my own adventure.

Our cart was half full of bags of items when we were finally done. I couldn't help chuckling at the strange looks we were getting from other shoppers.

"What else does this store have?" Fox asked, heading towards the nearest aisle.

"Yes, I'd like to see what else is here," Nico said, following Fox.

"Well, in that case, I'm going to get another cart," Ezio said. "Knowing you four, you're going to end up buying half of the store."

I didn't doubt it. "Just yell if you can't find us," I told him.

He scowled at me. "Jolie, I'm just going to follow your scent."

How had I forgotten that?

"Right," I said, smirking in embarrassment.

"Onward!" Deryn said, standing on one leg on the cart, then using the other to propel it forward again.

Rhys slipped his fingers into mine and tugged me close to his side. "Come on, beautiful. Let's go on an adventure."

I laughed. "The grocery store is hardly an adventure."

"We're exploring unfamiliar territories and leaving with treasures. Sounds like adventuring to me," he said.

I smirked. "Well, if this is an adventure, we already screwed up."

"How?" Rhys asked.

"We let our healer go first."

Rhys paused and then yelled, "Fox! Get back here!"

I laughed as we caught up to the other three, who had already filled the cart with several kinds of cereals and breakfast pastries.

"Sampling everything?" I asked.

They all nodded.

"After we figure out which of them are our favorites, we can order them in bulk," Fox explained.

"You realize there are like thirty more aisles and you've already filled the cart?" I said, smiling at the pure innocence they showed in situations like this.

"We can grab more carts if needed," Ezio said, pushing the new cart he brought into the middle of our group.

"Onward!" Rhys said. "We must continue our adventuring."

"Oh? Adventuring!" Fox said and smiled wide. "I'll stay in the middle in case we need healing."

"I've got the rear," Deryn said.

"I'm in front, Jolie behind me," Rhys said.

To anyone else, we must have sounded crazy, but this was our normal order when playing games together, and we easily fell into that mindset.

"Left," Rhys called over his shoulder.

We followed him to the left, down the next aisle.

"What's this?" Fox asked, picking up a can of frozen juice concentrate from the frozen bin.

"It's juice concentrate," I explained. "You put that in a container, and fill the container with water then mix it up, and you get juice."

His eyes widened, and he grabbed six different flavors, putting them in the second cart, which was already half full.

"This?" Deryn asked, holing up a box of frozen waffles.

"Frozen waffles," I said, smirking.

"You've never seen frozen waffles before?" Ezio asked Deryn.

Deryn shook his head. "So, you just heat them up?"

I nodded. "Microwave them or put them in a toaster."

"Get a bunch," Rhys said. "They'll make for a fast breakfast when we run behind."

Deryn nodded, and did as Rhys said.

"Is this really a pie?" Rhys asked, looking in the glass at the frozen chocolate pies.

"Yes. You just put them in the fridge to defrost, and eat when they're ready," I said.

"Get ten," Nico said.

I laughed and shook my head. "Where are you going to store all this frozen food?"

"We have a deep freeze in the kitchen," Rhys said.

I blinked in silence. "What? Since when?"

"We bought it last week," Nico answered.

"I totally missed that," I admitted.

"Ice cream!" Nico said, sounding like a giddy child.

"There are so many flavors!" Fox gasped.

"Get strawberry, please," I requested, staying by the cart so I was out of the way of their madness.

"I've never seen them like this before," Ezio whispered. He looked down at me. "You really do help them become more than they were."

"Stop," I said, blushing. "I'm just taking them shopping. Anyone could have done the same and had the same reactions from them."

He shook his head. "No. I don't think so, Jolie."

I didn't know what to say to that, but was saved because they headed to the next aisle, and I had to push the cart to catch up.

Our last aisle was the bread aisle.

Fox's eyes gleamed with joy. "So many different types!"

"Blueberry bagels and blueberry muffins for me," I requested.

Nico grabbed them for me, and then returned to staring at the bagels, a thoughtful expression on his face. "There's just so many different types and brands," he whispered.

"What about that aisle?" Rhys asked, pointing at the aisle across the way. "You had us skip it. Why?"

"That's the shampoo, hair dye, and feminine hygiene aisle. I didn't think you'd want to go down it," I explained.

"Do they have lots of shampoos?" Fox asked.

"With different scents?" Deryn asked.

Oh boy. Obviously, we were headed down the shampoo aisle.

"Yes, let's go."

They put their last bread choices in the cart, and then headed to the shampoo aisle. I watched with quiet fascination as they picked up various bottles, opened the lid, and took turns smelling the shampoos.

"That's disgusting!" Fox gagged. "Who would use that?"

"This one's not much better," Deryn said, holding a shampoo out to Fox.

Fox smelled it and gagged again.

"This one smells like Jolie," Nico said. The others reached for it, taking turns smelling it.

I smirked. "That's because that is the shampoo I use."

"Oh, smell this one," Rhys said, holding out a bottle that was covered in flower designs.

"Pretty," Fox said, tossing it into the cart. "I'm getting that."

"You're going to use flower scented shampoo?" I asked.

"Why not?" Fox asked, and all of them looked at me.

I raised my hands in surrender. "Nothing. It's fine. I was just asking."

They resumed smelling shampoos then moved to the conditioner and body washes next. I couldn't stand to see how much they spent, so I stood by the exit, with Ezio at my side.

"I'm hungry again," I complained. "I don't think I'm going to like being hungry so often."

He chuckled. "It just means you'll get to eat lots of delicious food."

"I want pizza," I said. "Pizza and chocolate."

"At the same time?" he asked.

I laughed, bending over to clutch at my stomach from the laughter tightening my stomach muscles. "No!"

He chuckled. "Well, I've heard of women eating lots of weird things while pregnant, so it wouldn't surprise me."

"Not this girl," I said with a smile. "At least, not yet."

The guys pushed the two overflowing shopping carts towards us.

"We're ready!" Fox said.

"I'm hungry," I announced, smiling.

"Well, then let's get the princess some food," Fox said.

CHAPTER 12

RHYS

"This is so good," Jolie moaned as she ate the last piece of the large pizza we'd gotten for her.

Deryn glanced at me, a smirk on his face. Yeah, she was already consuming more than she used to, now that she was pregnant.

"Do you want dessert?" Nico asked.

Jolie nodded, stuffing a pizza crust from Deryn's plate in her mouth.

I took a drink from my water to stop from laughing at her.

She was incredibly adorable, and I couldn't wait to see what she looked like with a cute, round belly.

"What?" Jolie asked, looking up at me.

Crap. She'd caught me staring.

"Nothing, beautiful. Just admiring you," I said.

She wiped her face with a napkin and frowned. "I'm eating a lot, aren't I?"

"No," I said immediately. "You need to eat twice what you normally do to get enough nourishment for the baby."

She scowled, her brows scrunching together into the most adorable face ever. "I still feel hungry, even though I already ate a lot."

"It's normal," Fox assured her, giving me a scowl.

My bad.

"Here, pick out dessert," Deryn said, setting a menu in front of her.

Her eyes lit up at the sight of the desserts, and she spent a solid minute in silence, deciding what she wanted.

"Chocolate cream pie," she said with a nod.

We all watched her eat it, our attentions focused on her, and that small spark of magic growing in her womb.

Whose would it be?

CHAPTER 13

JOLIE

Nico crawled out of bed, his movements slow, like he was trying not to wake me.

"Nico?" I asked, rubbing at my eyes. A glance at the clock confirmed it was still really early, only five in the morning.

He kissed my cheek. "I'm sorry. I didn't mean to wake you. I just need to go take care of something."

"You've been disappearing a lot lately. Where are you going?" I asked, standing to face him.

"It's nothing to worry about," he said, walking backwards, away from me. "I'll be back soon. The others are here to keep you company."

I reached out towards him just as he teleported away, my fingers brushing his shirt. His magic teleported him away, and when I looked down at my hand, a few of my fingers were missing.

I stared in disbelief, then screamed and clutched at my hand. Had part of my fingers teleported with Nico? I dropped to my knees and closed my eyes, crying out in agony.

"Jolie!" Fox yelled, grabbing my shoulders.

I wrenched my eyes open and stared up into Fox's face. I bolted upright and glanced at my hand, which was whole. I turned to my right and glared at the spot Nico was supposed to be in.

"Where's Nico?" I asked, snarling.

"He left a couple of minutes ago," Fox said. "What happened? Why were you screaming?"

A dream. It must have been a dream.

"I dreamt he was leaving and I touched him as he teleported, and it teleported part of my fingers with him," I said, clutching my hand to my chest as the phantom pains still lingered.

"Your fingers are all there and accounted for," Fox said, kissing the tip of each one.

"Where does Nico keep sneaking off to?" I demanded, climbing out of bed and heading to my dresser.

"What are you doing?" Rhys asked, sitting up and rubbing his eyes.

"I'm going to find Nico," I explained, and pulled on a pair of pants.

"He's just with the mages, taking care of king things," Deryn said. "Come back to bed."

"He doesn't have to sneak out, if that's all he is doing," I argued.

"He leaves early so that he is gone mostly while you're asleep. He doesn't like to be away from you, even with all of us here, and Ezio downstairs," Fox explained.

Ezio had moved in yesterday, at Dan's urging. He had decided that it was better for Ezio to be my permanent guard, despite me already having four permanent guards who slept in my bed.

I gave up, stripped off my pants, and climbed back into bed. When Nico came back, I would talk with him. I understood he had more duties now that he was king, but I did not like him sneaking off without telling me. Plus, I had a niggling feeling that there was more going on than the other guys knew with Nico.

After breakfast, I went to the room across from mine, the nursery, and stood with my hands on my hips as I surveyed the empty room. We'd ordered some furniture, but I still needed to figure out how I wanted to paint it.

Green? Green was a neutral color, that would work for either gender, since we didn't know what it was yet.

It. I hated calling the baby I was growing 'it,' but until I knew at least the race, that was all I could call the little parasite.

"What are you doing?" Ezio asked from the doorway.

I wasn't surprised he had come looking for me. I had been here at least five minutes.

"Debating what color to paint the nursery. What do you think about green?" I asked.

"I'm not giving my input. This isn't my child," he said. "I don't want to sway you in anyway."

"I need to talk to you," I said, turning to face him.

Ezio scowled and crossed his arms over his chest. "About?"

"I need you to promise me something," I said softly. I didn't want my mates overhearing our discussion, so I peeked out the room, and then shut the door.

"I'm listening, but not agreeing yet," he told me.

"I know it's a very unlikely chance…a super rare occurrence… but if I die during childbirth—"

"You're not going to die," he growled. "We're going to have the top healers with you and—"

"Ezio!" I yelled, my eyes no doubt glowing with my anger. "Listen!"

His mouth snapped shut.

"If that happens, my mates are going to be beside themselves with grief. I need you to promise that you'll take care of the baby until they're sane again. Okay? The healers will be focused on me, and my mates won't be themselves, so I need someone I can trust who will focus on the baby." My voice cracked at the end, which I hated. I exhaled, trying to ease my worry. "Please, Ezio. I need you to do this. I need you to promise me that if something happens to me, the baby will be safe."

His arms had dropped during my explanation, and now he used them to hug me. "I promise," he whispered, stroking my hair. "I'll take care of the baby."

I hugged him back, wiping my tears off on his shirt. "Thank you."

"But, you're not going to die," he grumbled.

"Okay," I said with a nod. "I'll try my hardest."

"What's wrong?" Rhys asked, his voice more dragon than man.

"Nothing," I said. "Just worrying about the future."

Rhys looked at Ezio, but Ezio refused to meet his eyes, looking down at the floor instead.

"Jolie," Rhys growled.

I slipped my arms around his waist and rested my head on his chest. "I love you, Puff."

His anger melted away, and he wrapped me up in his arms. "I love you, too."

"Food?" I asked.

He chuckled. "Yeah, I've got some snacks for you."

"Yum!" I said, grabbed his hand, and dragged him after me so he couldn't grill Ezio.

Ezio followed on our heels, his brows furrowed, but he remained silent. Even if he told Rhys or Deryn, I didn't care. I needed to know someone would focus on the baby, and it honestly relieved some of my stress.

"What's on the agenda for today?" I asked.

"A trip to the elves," Rhys answered.

We entered the dining room, and Fox stood to kiss my cheek and pull out my chair.

"What are we doing at the elves'?" I asked

"Uh, finding out the baby's race," Fox said, his body tense. "Did you forget?"

"I didn't realize it was happening today," I admitted. "Did you tell me?"

They all nodded.

I exhaled. "Sorry." I had been extremely forgetful lately.

"Have you been taking your pills?" Fox asked.

I chewed on the inside of my lip. "No."

He sighed. "Jolie, you know you're supposed to take them."

"They make me nauseous," I said, filling my plate with food from the table. Deryn must have cooked, since there were several types of meat on the table and that was his normal cooking procedure. Lots of meat, one type of vegetable, and several types of carbs.

"They are to ensure you and the baby are healthy," Rhys growled. "You have to take them."

"Whatever," I grumbled, but knew they were right. I tried to take them with and without food, but they always made me nauseous. "Maybe Kara will know some way for me to take them that won't make me want to throw up."

As soon as I finished eating, we all climbed into an SUV, and drove to the main house of the elves.

Katar and Kara met us outside, both hugging me and kissing my cheeks.

"Are you ready?" Kara asked.

"No," I mumbled. "Nico isn't here."

"Of course I am," Nico said from the doorway of the house, smiling.

I gave him my best glare. "You are in so much trouble."

His smile slipped. "What? Why?"

"Later," I growled then exhaled and calmed myself. "Okay, let's get this over with."

"You act like it's a terrible thing," Katar said, laughing.

"It could be," I muttered as I walked by him into the house.

Kara had a room on the side of the house that she used for healing. She had a nice bed, that had decent padding. I started to climb up on it, but Rhys picked me up, and set me on it.

"I can do it," I growled.

"I know, but I don't want you straining," he said.

"I'm not *that* pregnant," I said and sighed.

"Lay back," Kara ordered me.

I obeyed, and two of my mates stood on each side of me.

She carried a weird looking wand and held it over my belly. "Ready?" she asked.

I nodded. All four of my mates nodded.

She whispered something, and the wand began to glow. The glow spread to my stomach, and then five colors rose into the air.

"What?" she said, frowning.

"What's wrong?" I asked.

"It's only supposed to show two colors," Katar said.

"Try again," Fox said.

"Let me help this time," Katar offered.

Kara grumbled something below her breath, but let Katar help, his hand on the wand too, and his power mixing with hers.

The same five colors rose again.

"What the hell?" Deryn asked.

"Is that possible?" Rhys asked Kara, his brows furrowed.

"No, but we are talking about Jolie," she said and chuckled. "This girl always takes what is possible and tosses it out the window."

"Explain, please," I begged.

"It's supposed to show us two colors, the color of the being you're impregnated by and your color. But, it's showing colors for all of us," Nico said.

"Which would mean the baby is a mixture of me and the four of you?" I asked.

They nodded.

I was glad I was lying down. I relaxed on the bed, and stared up at the ceiling.

"Oh, dear," a female voice whispered.

We all spun, staring at my mother in her ghostly form.

"Mom?" I asked.

"Mom?" Kara asked. She looked at my mother and her eyes widened. "You're dead."

Mom smiled. "Hi, Kara. Long time no see."

"Don't you dare—" Kara began, but Katar grabbed her.

"What did you do?" I asked my mother.

"I fiddled with your hormones a bit, to help you get pregnant, and—"

"Mom!" I gasped. "Why would you do that? I wasn't planning to get pregnant yet. I wanted to kill our enemies first and—"

"There's never a right time to have a baby," she said. "Right, Kara?"

"Don't you talk to me," Kara growled.

"Aw, don't be like that. I really am dead. I only come back when I can convince the goddess to give me a few minutes with Jolie."

"So, you did this?" I asked.

She nodded. "You were so worried about who the father was going to be. This way, the baby is all of yours." She smiled, so proud of herself.

"Well, it does take away the stress you have been holding in," Nico said.

"Now we're just going to have to worry about how the baby will turn out," Fox mumbled.

"It'll be just like Jolie," Mom said. "It will be able to use all of your powers, and will be incredibly powerful."

"Have you been haunting Dad?" I asked.

She smirked. "Occasionally."

"He didn't have something to do with this, did he?" I asked.

She shrugged, but didn't respond.

"Of course," I said and sighed.

"I have to go," Mom said, then rested her hand on my stomach. "This baby is going to be glorious. And you're going to be a wonderful mother."

Tears brimmed in my eyes, and she kissed my forehead before disappearing.

"Well, that explains that," Katar said, smiling wide. "Now I really can't wait to play with my grandchild."

A hybrid.

I stared up at the ceiling and then started laughing. I laughed until I had to clutch my stomach.

"What?" Deryn asked.

"I've got one of the weirdest lives ever! I became the queen to the four princes when I drunkenly stumbled into a meeting, and ended the war by handing over a necklace from my grandma. Then I became your mates. Now, my dead mother is meddling in our affairs, and created a hybrid baby to make me happy." I laughed again, wiping at the tears coming from my eyes.

Everyone in the room laughed.

"Well, no one can say being mated to you is dull or uneventful," Fox said, smiling wide.

That was definitely true. Though, I wasn't certain that was a good thing.

CHAPTER 14

NICO

R hys, Fox, Deryn, and I stood together in Fox's old bedroom in his parents' house. Jolie and Kara were talking, so it gave us a perfect chance to hide.

"We're going to have to isolate her," Rhys said.

Sadly, he was right.

"If the others find out she's having a hybrid, it could be chaos," Fox whispered. He looked at his wall, as though he could see through it, and see Jolie. "She's not going to like us hiding her away, even more than we have been."

"It's necessary to keep her safe," I said. "She'll hate us for a bit, but once our baby is born, she will thank us for it."

"Have you learned anything new?" Deryn asked me.

"About what?" I asked, scowling.

He gave me his, don't-act-stupid look. "Our enemies."

Did he know? Did they know?

"Nothing more than you know," I said and shrugged.

"So, you've been sneaking out and still haven't found anything useful?" Rhys asked, folding his arms over his chest.

Shit.

"How did you know?" I asked.

They all rolled their eyes.

"We've known you our whole lives, Nico," Fox said. "You can't hide shit from us. Jolie is pretty suspicious, too."

"Yeah. Be prepared for a lecture when we get home," Deryn said with a smirk.

Great.

"We're still no closer to finding them," I admitted.

"Maybe it is better if we stop looking," Rhys said.

All eyes turned to him. Rhys, the take charge guy, wanted to sit back?

"What brought this on?" I asked.

"Maybe, if we leave them alone for a bit, they will leave us alone. If we can keep Jolie out of harm's way long enough for her to have our baby, I would feel a lot better. I'm all for blowing them to smithereens, but her safety is our top priority. I just want the baby born without any issues."

"So, you want me to stop?" I asked. I knew I was scowling, but I wanted to find Justina. She'd severed our bonds and tortured Jolie, and I could not forgive her for that. I needed to find her and then tear her to pieces.

"For now," Rhys said with a nod.

"I agree," Deryn said.

"Same," Fox said.

I sighed and rubbed my temples. "Fine. Until she has the baby, we will lay low."

"Should we get more guards for the house?" Fox asked.

Now we were all looking at him.

"You think she needs more than the four of us, Ezio, Leona, and Thor since he is basically always over?" Deryn asked.

He shrugged. "It couldn't hurt to have one more from each of our clans, right? One more dragon, elf, and mage could make a huge difference."

"I don't want another mage," I said. "It will interfere with my ability to sense magic users."

"Okay, so another dragon and elf," Fox said.

"I bet Andras would be more than willing to come protect her," Deryn said.

I thought he was teasing Rhys at first, but then I realized he was serious.

"Really?" I asked.

Deryn nodded. "He flirts with her to rile Rhys up, but he really does care for her."

"Who would you bring?" I asked Fox.

He shrugged. "Not sure, but I can find someone."

"I'll ask Andras," Rhys agreed. "He has grown fond of her, so I know he'll do everything he can to keep her safe."

"If shit hits the fan, I'm calling in her exes," Fox said.

"No," Rhys growled.

Fox met his glare with one of his own. "Stop being a jealous ass and think about it. Who would be better to protect her than men who are in love with her? It's already programmed into them to protect her. When they see her with a child that's part of their race, their instincts will override any other thought."

He was right.

"Only if it is absolutely necessary," I agreed.

Fox nodded once.

"So, are we going to make a list of names we want her to consider for the baby?" Deryn asked, smiling wide.

"I've got one for a girl and one for a boy all ready," Fox said.

"How is she going to choose?" I asked.

"Draw from a hat?" Rhys asked, beaming.

This was what I had hoped for the first time I saw her with all of us. There was something special about Jolie, and I just knew that she would end up making us smile like fools. I had been right.

On more than one occasion, the four of us had felt joy above anything else we had ever experienced. We had also felt pain, but the joy was worth it. Our mate was pregnant. My mate was pregnant. I was going to be a dad.

Even though it was probably terrible of me, I was glad my father wasn't alive for this. He would have blown a gasket when he found out our child was a hybrid. It was bad enough Jolie was a siren, now we would have a siren, mage, dragon, wolf, elf as a child.

"We better get back to her, before she gets anxious," Fox said.

We nodded in agreement, and filed out of the room.

CHAPTER 15

JOLIE

"More guards?" I asked, mouth hanging open as Andras hugged me.

"Just two more," Rhys said. "And, does Andras really count?"

Andras rested his hand on my stomach, which was already much larger than a month ago when I'd found out I was pregnant. The baby kicked at his hand, and Andras smiled.

"I'm just here to make sure nothing happens to my favorite sister-in-law, and my niece or nephew," Andras said, and kissed my cheek.

I grumbled, but he pulled me deeper into the house, to the dining room where everyone was gathered for dinner. Andras had shown up, and I'd come to see why he was here. We stepped into the room, and I stared at Silverowl, Fox's brother sitting next to Fox. His silver hair was braided along his skull, and secured in a ponytail on the back.

"Silver, what are you doing here?" I asked, walking to him.

He stood, and kissed me on the cheek. "My brother requested I come to keep you safe. I couldn't turn him down."

I glared at Fox. "Why do you guys keep doing things without asking me?"

He smiled. "Because we know you'll say no."

I growled, and the baby tumbled around inside my stomach, making me cringe and grip the back of Silver's chair.

"The baby's acting up again?" Fox asked.

"Yeah," I grumbled.

Fox rested his hand on my stomach, and the baby kicked his hand. Fox chuckled. "That feels wolf-ish to me."

Deryn immediately stood, walked to me, and put his hand in place of Fox's. The baby gently kicked his hand, and then stilled.

Somehow, the guys had figured out how to tell when one aspect of the baby's nature was acting up over the other. I couldn't tell the difference, which really bothered me.

"Spunky," Deryn whispered. He bent down, and placed his forehead against my stomach. I felt the baby move, and press against Deryn's forehead, but it wasn't a kick. It was like the baby was trying to mimic him, though I couldn't be too sure of that.

"When do you find out the gender?" Andras asked. He'd taken a seat while the baby had distracted me.

"Next month," Fox said.

"Do you have a name picked?" Silver asked.

I shook my head. "Not yet." The guys had given me their top choices for each gender the other night. I had purchased a white board, put it in the nursery, and wrote down all the names we were deciding between, separated by gender, on it. It made it easier for me to view them all at once. I'd gone in there a few times, and said the names while resting my hand on my stomach, but the baby hadn't reacted to any of them. Not that I genuinely thought it would, but it would have made my life easier.

Deryn pulled out my chair for me, and I sat down, immediately digging into the plate of food before me. The baby made me eat a lot now, even more than I had a month ago. I finished three plates of food, then two pieces of cake before I was finally full.

Andras walked beside me to the living room, staring at my stomach.

"What?" I asked.

"Just curious what the baby is going to look like," he admitted.

I sighed. "You and me both."

"Well, it's definitely going to be attractive," Deryn said, and draped an arm around my shoulders.

"Or, we could be that attractive couple that has an ugly kid," I said.

Deryn scoffed and rolled his eyes. "Not a chance."

"I still can't believe your dead mother interfered with your pregnancy," Andras whispered. "You guys have the craziest lives ever."

I sighed again, something I did a lot lately. "Yeah, I know."

Leona skipped down the stairs, and pulled me away from Deryn. "How's my favorite prego?"

"Pregnant and tired," I admitted.

"Come sit," she ordered me, pulling me to the living room, and to the love seat. She wrapped us both up in a fluffy, quilted blanket up to our chins, then smiled at the guys. "We should watch a movie."

"What do you want to watch?" I asked.

"Comedy?" she suggested.

"Definitely no romance movies," Fox said.

"Hey! It was sad!" I snapped at him, knowing he was saying that because the last time we'd watched a romance, I had bawled for an hour afterwards.

"No romances," Rhys agreed.

"What about action?" Andras asked.

"I'm up for an action flick," I agreed.

"Me, too," Leona agreed. She moved closer to me and smiled. "I have so many movies to make up for missing."

Growing up in Atlantis, she didn't get to see movies, or really anything, since they didn't have television, cable, or the internet down there. I was still trying to figure out how to get those things down to them. There had to be a way.

"I'll pick," Andras said, squatting down by our movie shelf, which was really a wall of shelves lined with movies. Fox and Nico had organized it by genre, and then alphabetically. There had to be at least one thousand movies, most likely more than that. It was an insanely massive collection built by the five of us merging our collections into one.

"Popcorn?" I asked.

"And candy!" Leona agreed.

"On it!" Fox said, heading to the kitchen.

"I'm so spoiled," I said with a happy sigh.

"Yes, you are, but you deserve it," Leona said, and rested her head on my shoulder.

Someone knocked on the door, and then Thor came into the living room. He kissed Leona on the cheek and sat on the floor in front of her.

"Hey, Thor," I said, smiling.

He glanced up at me and smiled. "Hey, Jo."

Fox returned, set up a tray with the snacks, and then sat on the floor in front of me. "Ready," he told Andras.

Andras nodded, and hit play. The rest of the guys took seats on the couches, or on the floor. Deryn shifted into his wolf form, and lay next to Fox, who occasionally tossed him a piece of popcorn, which Deryn caught in his wolf mouth.

I munched on popcorn, candy, and cuddled with my best friend, surrounded by my favorite guys. It was the perfect night.

When the movie finished, Deryn chose another one, and more popcorn was made. Nico stole me from Leona, cuddling with me on the couch with Rhys to our left. Thor took my vacated spot, and pulled Leona into his side with an arm around her shoulders.

I couldn't help smiling as I watched them feed each other popcorn. They were adorable together.

Halfway through the movie, someone pounded on our door, startling everyone in the room. Deryn, Rhys, and Andras left the room to investigate.

A moment later, Dan walked in, scowling. "You've been keeping her from me," Dan growled.

"No, we've just been staying home," Deryn argued.

"Which is keeping her from me," Dan growled. He looked around the room until he spotted me. Then he picked me up and hugged me, but much gentler than he usually did.

"Hi, Father," I said, smiling.

"I've come to commune with my grandchild," he said, and set me down.

"What?" I asked.

"He wants to talk to the baby," Deryn explained.

Dan got down on his knees and then sat back on his heels, trying to lower himself enough to reach my stomach, but he was still too tall, so he bent forward. He rested his hand on my stomach, and I felt the power zap him through my stomach. He snarled, but then immediately smiled. He leaned forward and whispered to my stomach, too softly for me to hear. The baby swirled around in my stomach, moving much faster than before.

"What are you telling the baby?" I asked. "I haven't felt it move so much."

"Just promising to spoil the little hybrid once released into the world," he said. He pressed his forehead to my stomach, just like Deryn had done, and I felt the baby lean into him the same way. Had Dan done this with Deryn when Deryn was still inside his mother? Was this how their bonds started?

"It's already quite strong," Dan whispered.

Everyone was watching and stayed silent as Dan spoke.

"You're going to have your hands full, son. There is zero doubt that this little hybrid will be an alpha. Zero doubt," Dan said and stood. He rested his hand on my cheek and smiled. "You're glowing, daughter. Pregnancy looks great on you."

I blushed and rubbed my now calm stomach. "Thank you."

"This is why you came here?" Nico asked.

"It's a bonding thing," Dan said.

"Which is why we're all here," Katar said.

Dan stepped aside so I could see past his bulky frame. Katar, Kara, Emrys, and Adelaide stood in the doorway of the living room.

"What does this do?" Nico asked.

With his father being dead, and his mother being human, I wasn't surprised that he didn't know what the purpose was. I was glad I wasn't the only one in the dark.

"The more often a king or alpha interact with a fetus, the stronger the fetus is," Adelaide explained. "It ensures there are no miscarriages and that the baby is born healthy."

"Since this is a hybrid, we want to be sure we take every precautionary measure possible," Kara said.

"You guys could have told us," Fox grumbled.

"We hadn't thought we would need to," Katar said. "We didn't realize you were going to hide Jolie even from us."

"We didn't want to risk the car rides," Rhys explained.

"You have a mage," Adelaide said, pointing at Nico.

"It isn't worth the risk," Rhys said and shrugged.

Adelaide glared at him. "Visiting your family isn't worth the risk?" she asked.

"Addy, don't give your son a hard time," Emrys said. He walked to me, smiling, and then hugged me lightly. "How are you feeling?"

"Good, thanks," I replied as I hugged him back.

"May I?" he asked.

I nodded. I had quickly gotten over them touching my stomach. Most Others liked touching in general, and being able to touch my stomach was top of their priorities.

"You sure you don't want me to move Martin and his family in here?" Dan asked Deryn. "Sharla can help Jolie if she goes into labor too early, and it wouldn't hurt to have another male here."

"Thanks, Dad, but Andras and Silverowl are helping us now," Deryn said.

"Hello, blessed child," Emrys whispered to my stomach. He rested his hand on it, and immediately the baby zapped him. Emrys chuckled. "You weren't joking, Dan. This is one feisty baby."

"Just like the momma," Dan said, smiling proudly.

Emrys rested his forehead against my stomach, and once again, the baby pressed forward.

How strange was it that the unborn child would know what to do?

"My turn," Adelaide said, shoving Emrys aside. She kissed my cheek, then knelt and began whispering quickly to the baby. The baby did a few somersaults, then she pressed her forehead to my stomach and the baby met her.

By the time all of them were done, I was crying.

Fox wiped my face with his sleeve, and hugged me.

"How often do you need to do this?" I asked, sniffling.

"We would prefer at least once a week," Dan said.

"Okay," I agreed, and wiped my face on Fox's shoulder.

"You need a milkshake," Kara said, smiling wide.

"Oh, yes!" Adelaide said. "She definitely needs a milkshake. Do you have ice cream?"

I nodded.

"Come, Kara. Let's make our daughter-in-law a milkshake," Adelaide said, looping her arm through Kara's. I was glad that Adelaide didn't feel the need to test me anymore. Now I wasn't on high alert all the time around her.

"We'll be right back," Kara called over her shoulder as they left.

"They enjoy having someone to fuss over," Emrys said, smirking. "Let's hope your pregnancy goes well, or she might decide to move in."

"Sit," Dan commanded me and guided me back to Nico who hadn't moved.

I sat beside Nico, and he kissed my temple.

"So, what are we watching?" Dan asked, sitting down on my left.

Deryn told him the name and then went to the kitchen to make more popcorn. Our group grew larger, as the parents of my guys joined us to finish the movie. Kara and Adelaide brought everyone milkshakes, and as soon as I took one sip, I moaned.

"We added some vitamins to it as well," Kara said. "To help you and the baby. So, it's actually a healthy milkshake."

"Can I have one of these every day?" I asked Nico.

He chuckled. "I'm sure they'll be willing to give us the recipe."

"Or, we could just make them every time we come over," Kara said in a singsong voice.

"Once-a-week milkshakes are fine with me," I said quickly, which made everyone laugh.

We returned to our companionable silence, only broken when something in the movie was funny and some would laugh.

What would it be like if my father was here? Would he get along with the other kings and the queens? I wanted to visit him, but I knew the guys would not let me travel that far when they wouldn't even let me travel to their parents' clans.

"What's wrong?" Dan asked, wiping a tear that had fallen down my cheek away.

"Just missing my dad," I admitted.

"I haven't talked to him in years," Emrys said.

"Me, neither," Dan agreed.

"We could invite him here," Fox offered. "I'm sure Sam can hold down Atlantis until he returns."

"I doubt he would come," I said, biting my lip.

"He'll want to come bond with the baby," Emrys said, and Dan and Katar nodded in agreement.

"Oh, are we bonding with the baby now?" Mom asked as she appeared in front of us.

"What?" Dan asked.

"You really are real," Emrys said.

Adelaide stood, hands fisted, and glared at mom. "You visit your daughter, but not your best friend?"

Best friend? My mother and Adelaide had been best friends?

Mom smiled. "Oh, Addy. I'm dead, silly. I'm meddling much more than I should be anyway."

"Yeah, about that," Dan said. "What are you doing meddling with your daughter and the baby?"

She glared at Dan. "Shush, Daniel. I do what I want."

"Obviously," he muttered.

"Mom," I said with an exasperated sigh.

She walked to me and then instead of resting her hand on my stomach, she slipped her incorporeal hand through my stomach. The baby shimmied, and then stilled a moment, before doing several somersaults.

"What did you do?" I asked.

"Just checked to make sure everything is going well. Our little bundle of joy is perfect. I can't wait for you to see him or her," she said and smirked.

"You know!" I gasped.

She shrugged. "Maybe."

"What is it?" I asked.

"Nope," she said and shook her head. "I've meddled too much." She blew me a kiss. "Love you."

Before I could open my mouth, she disappeared. I roared angrily. "You can't just come and go as you please! Ugh!"

"Technically, she can," Dan whispered.

I turned my glare on him, and he just smiled.

"Alright, I think that's enough excitement for Jolie for the night," Nico said. He put his arm around my shoulders, then teleported me to our room.

"What's wrong?" I asked.

He knelt in front of me, and whispered to the baby. Again, too low for me to hear. Then, he rested his forehead against my stomach. It took a minute, but the baby met him, and I felt Nico's joy through our bond.

"What's it feel like?" I asked him.

"It doesn't have a voice, yet I feel like it's communicating with me. I don't know how to explain it. But, I can feel the magic within it. It is going to be very strong." He stood, smiling, and kissed me lightly on the lips.

"Are you alright?" I asked.

"I'm just tired. I have a lot going on with the mages and the war. And, with our baby," he said.

"Anything I can do to help?" I asked, resting my right hand on his left cheek.

He set his hand over mine. "Cuddle with me?"

I smiled wide and climbed up onto the bed. He followed me, flopping down onto his back. On my side, I snuggled up to him, resting my head on his chest, and threw a leg over his legs.

He stroked his fingers up and down my side, and kissed the top of my head.

"This is my favorite place to be," he whispered and exhaled loudly.

"Hey! They're cuddling without us!" Fox said as he entered the room.

I raised my head to tell them to give us some time, but Nico patted the bed. "Come on, you pathetic little kit. Get in here."

Fox shifted into his fox form, leapt up onto the bed, and snuggled with his head resting on my neck. His fur was really soft, and his whiskers tickled the bottom of my chin.

"Cuddle puddle!" Deryn yelled, and charged into the room.

117

He shifted into his wolf form, and spooned himself around my butt, resting his head on Nico's legs.

Rhys came in and scowled. "This is incredibly unfair."

Fox crawled over the top of me, being careful not to step on me, and lay across Nico's chest, resting his head on my neck again, but from the opposite side. Deryn moved down a bit, so Rhys had enough room to spoon me from behind.

Once Rhys was settled, everyone let out a collective sigh.

"My favorite place," I whispered, and leaned up to kiss Nico on the cheek.

"Are the parents gone?" Nico asked.

"Yes," Rhys said. "They all left."

"So, we can sleep now?" I asked, my eyelids already growing heavy.

"Yes, my queen. Go to sleep," Rhys whispered, and kissed my shoulder.

CHAPTER 16

JOLIE

"**D**ad!" Deryn roared, startling us all from our sleep.

At some point during the night, he'd shifted back into his human form.

"What is it?" I asked.

Deryn turned the light on, and put some clothes on. "Dad's hurt."

"How do you know?" I asked, climbing out of bed.

"I can feel it," Deryn growled.

I started to get dressed, but Rhys took my hands. "No."

"Dan—"

"No," Deryn growled. "Rhys, stay with her. If this is a trick, we need someone who can fly her away."

Nico and Fox had gotten dressed already, and Nico had his staff in hand. Fox and Deryn rested their hands on Nico's shoulder, and they teleported away.

"Andras, Ezio, and Silver," Rhys called.

All three appeared at the doorway the next moment.

"Secure the border," Rhys ordered them.

"Attack?" Ezio asked.

"Dan's injured. It could be a distraction, but we aren't sure yet," Rhys said.

Rhys waited until they were gone and then held out the clothes I had started to put on.

"Oh, now I can change?" I asked, but I knew why he had stopped me before. I changed and sat on the bed.

Rhys stood, his back rigid as he waited for the others to return and report. Several minutes later, they still hadn't returned. "Shit," he said. "Leona! Thor!"

Thor appeared in the doorway, holding Leona. "Yes?"

"I think we're under attack," Rhys said.

"Roof?" Thor asked.

Rhys picked me up, and then nodded. "Yes."

We raced to the roof, but paused at the door.

"Stay," Thor ordered Leona and set her down next to me. He shifted into his warrior's form, held his hammer in one hand, and pushed open the door. He darted out onto the roof, then a moment later came back. "Ten dhampirs to the south. They're fighting the three others. They're winning."

"Who is winning?" I asked, the blood pounding in my ears.

"Our side," Thor said.

"I'll fly the girls out. You go assist them," Rhys said.

"I don't need to be protected," Leona argued.

"I'm not protecting you," Rhys explained. "I want you to be with us to protect Jolie in case Trident Douche shows up."

That got her attention. She kissed Thor deeply and whispered, "Stay safe."

He kissed her forehead. "You, too."

Rhys set me down, shifted into his dragon form, and then waited as Leona and I climbed onto his back. As soon as we were settled, he took to the sky, circling higher and higher above the house.

I could see the others finally, and let out a breath. There were only five dhampirs left, and our side didn't appear wounded.

"This seems too small," Leona said. "Why only send ten dhampirs if they have an army?" she asked Rhys.

Rhys snarled, and then roared as something hit his neck. Whatever it was had bounced off his dragon scales, but it proved the ten weren't the only ones.

"Fly!" I ordered Rhys, fear making my order more of a scream.

He obeyed, flying away from the roof. As we flew over the trees, I saw the huge number of enemies swarming towards our house.

"They're not going to survive!" I told Rhys.

"Put a bubble around Rhys's head," Leona ordered me.

I did as she said, putting a silencing bubble around his head, so his ears were covered.

Leona inhaled, then began singing. The song was a haunting melody, full of loss and sorrow. The enemies below turned away from the house, and started following us.

I extended the bubble to cover me, so I could talk to Rhys. "Rhys! Take us to the dragon's den!" I ordered him, and then made the bubble small again.

He banked left, following my orders. Leona continued to sing, her eyes closed as she used magic.

We arrived at the dragon's border, and Mawrth roared at us.

"What does that mean?" Leona asked, stopping in her singing.

"It means, we're in trouble," I said and released the bubble.

Mawrth and Emrys flew past us, their jaws snapped open, and fire poured out, covering the dhampirs who had been lured with us.

"Andras is fighting at the house!" I yelled to Mawrth. "He needs help!"

Mawrth roared at me.

I glared at him. "Do as I say! Go help your brother or I swear,

I will tear every single one of your scales from your body, while Rhys holds you down!"

Mawrth's eyes widened, and then he turned to obey.

"Dang, girl," Leona said and chuckled.

"He was long overdue for me to put him in his place. I have a feeling I'm going to have to fight him for dominance before he relinquishes," I said.

Rhys snarled.

"No, you can't get involved. It's my fight. Besides, your brother is super slow," I said.

Rhys growled again.

"Just take us to the house," I said and rolled my eyes at Leona.

"You realize that I have no idea what he said, right?" she asked, smirking.

"How are you feeling?" I asked Leona.

"Tired, but I'm okay. Just need to rest my voice a bit."

"Then shut up," I said and laughed.

Emrys roared as he approached us.

"Dan's hurt. My other mates went to the werewolves. There was a large group of dhampirs attacking the house, but Leona lured most of them here," I explained.

Emrys snorted smoke.

"I don't know if the others were attacked or not," I admitted. "Did you have any attacks?"

He snorted again.

"That's a no," I told Leona with a smirk.

I pulled out my phone and dialed Kara. She answered immediately. "We weren't attacked. I'm on my way to Dan. It's not good, Jolie. Get to the pack as soon as you can."

"Dan! Take me to Dan!" I screamed at Rhys.

He turned, and Emrys flew closer, then shifted into his human form, dropping down onto Rhys's back beside me.

"What about your—"

"Adelaide is there. She's a force to be reckoned with. And,

there are several of our strongest fighters posted nearby in case she happens to need help," he said. He looped his arm around me, and pulled me against his side. "You're too stressed. Try to calm down, please."

I relaxed against him, and sniffled. "I can't lose Dan."

He patted my shoulder. "Kara is on her way. She'll take care of him."

I hoped she arrived soon enough. Dan was like a second father to me. I didn't want to lose him. I couldn't think about losing him.

We flew into the werewolves' territory and to the house. Dan lay outside the house, with the pack standing in a loose circle around him.

Rhys landed just on the outside of the group, and I leapt down from him, charging through the group to get to Dan.

Deryn caught my shoulder, stopping me from going all the way to him.

There was a puddle of blood beneath Dan, and he had a hole in his stomach where I could see his intestines.

I turned and looked up at Deryn, not surprised that his eyes were wolf eyes. "What happened?"

"Dhampirs attacked. Hundreds of them," Deryn said, his voice more growl than human. "He killed a lot of them, but they came after the twins and he got hurt protecting them."

"Are they—"

"They're fine," Deryn said. He pulled me back into a hug, and rested his chin on top of my head.

"You're always such trouble," Kara grumbled to Dan as she healed him. "Can't you ever do anything halfway? I mean, you could have at least left your guts inside of your body for me."

"Sorry, Kara," Dan whispered. "I just know how much you love seeing intestines."

She huffed.

"Can I—" I started to ask.

Kara nodded. "Come, Jolie."

I moved forward, and sat next to Dan, avoiding his blood puddle. "Hello, Father. You're looking a bit pale," I said, trying to lighten the mood.

He smiled, and I slid my hand into his. "What are you doing here? You should be at home, where it's safe," he said.

"Our house was attacked, too," I explained. "And, I had to come see how you were. You've got a grandchild on the way, and he needs your expert spoiling."

Dan smiled, but closed his eyes. "I can't wait to meet your child. I'm going to spoil the hell out of that baby. It will have everything it wants, and will have the run of the pack."

I sniffled. "I'd have it no other way."

He had stopped bleeding, and new skin was beginning to grow over his stomach.

"Tell me, how you kings were all friends, yet at war with each other for so long?" I asked him.

He sighed. "I didn't want to be at war. I was against it from the beginning. But, the artifact is precious to us."

"It belongs to all three of you, though, right?" I asked.

"Yes. It actually belongs to Jinla. It helps protect us from things like demon portals. They still happen occasionally, but it is much harder for demons to enter Jinla now that the artifact is back in its rightful place," Dan explained.

"So, despite being at war, you guys managed to stay friends?"

"Yes. It was all due to everyone accusing each other of stealing the artifact. I tried several times to end the war, but they're a bunch of stubborn old men."

"Hey," Emrys barked.

Dan smiled. "Trespassing again?"

Emrys snorted. "I escorted our daughter here. I couldn't let her come unprotected."

"She was with me," Rhys said.

"More is better," Emrys said, dismissing his son.

"Have you picked names yet?" Dan asked and opened his eyes. Most of his stomach was closed with new skin now.

I shook my head. "Not yet. We have a board with the options listed, but I haven't been able to narrow it down yet."

"That was Milly's favorite part of being pregnant," Dan whispered. "She liked figuring out names, and then narrowing it down. She made a game of it."

Milly was Deryn's mother.

"How did she make a game of it?" I asked, rubbing the back of Dan's hand as Kara continued to heal him.

"She would pick five of the names, tell me them, and I would say pass or veto," he explained. "The ones I vetoed, she got a chance to argue for. The ones that passed, she wrote down on a new list. We had over one hundred names picked for Deryn in the beginning. It took us almost the entire pregnancy to settle on Deryn," Dan said. He turned his head to look at me and smiled. "She would have loved you, Jolie. You're exactly the type of woman she wanted for Deryn."

I blushed. "I wish I could have met her."

Dan nodded and then cringed.

"No moving," Kara snapped at him.

"Sorry, Kara," he whispered. "I know she would have loved to meet you. She did know your mother, though."

"Apparently everyone knows her," I mumbled.

"She was such a fiery woman. She didn't take crap from anyone, and that was what caught your dad's eye. Back before I was alpha, there was a nasty alpha in charge. He shifted into warrior form to try to intimidate your mom."

"It didn't work?" I asked.

He shook his head, laughter in his eyes. "She walked right up to him, his seven-foot-tall form towering above her, kicked him in the shin, and then sang him asleep."

I wish I could have seen that.

"Your father watched it happen, and within the next hour, he had asked her for a date," Dan said.

"She turned him down," Kara said, smiling. "She said just because he was royalty didn't mean she was going to bow to him and fawn over him."

"Oh, he told me about that," Dan said. "He said that was the moment he knew it was true love."

I chuckled.

"Sounds like someone else we know," Rhys said.

I stuck my tongue out at him and turned back to Dan. "So, Father, do you have any name suggestions?"

"Hey! He gets to offer names, but I don't?" Emrys demanded.

"I'm dying, of course I get extra benefits," Dan said.

"You're not dying," Kara said, rolling her eyes. "But, you would have if I hadn't shown up."

"Well?" I asked Dan.

He was silent a long time, and I thought he had fallen asleep, except his eyes were open.

"Sierra for a girl," he said. "And, Dameon for a boy."

"What is it with you and D names for boys?" Deryn asked.

Dan smirked, rolling his head to the side to look at his son. "Ladies love the d."

The sexual joke was so out of the blue that I burst into laughter, laughing so hard that I cried.

Kara sighed. "Laughing like that only encourages them, Jolie."

"I'm sorry, but that was hilarious," I said, wiping at the tears beneath my eyes.

Kara sighed. "I understand a bit better how you fit in with those four."

"Hey," Fox said. "What's that supposed to mean?"

She smiled. "I love you, Son."

Fox grumbled something, and Nico smiled while patting him on the back.

"So, what are we going to do now?" I asked.

"We're going to send more guards to your house, put up some major wards, and put you on lock down until our little bundle of joy is born," Dan said.

I wanted to argue. I would have argued, but I was okay with that.

"Okay," I said with a nod.

The baby started kicking, and kicked my rib really hard, making me gasp.

Dan reached up and set his hand on my stomach. "Easy, child. Your mom has had all the excitement she needs for one day."

The baby quieted, bumping Dan's hand once before going silent.

"You guys are like baby gurus," I whispered appreciatively.

Dan chuckled. "No, I could just smell the wolf on you."

"What?" I asked, looking at my mates.

"Sometimes it's strong enough we can smell it," Deryn agreed.

"Other times, once we touch you, we can sense what it is," Fox said.

"That's so weird," I whispered, looking down at my stomach.

"Alright, everyone back to their houses!" Deryn ordered the still-gathered werewolves.

They disbursed immediately, and Emrys walked over to help Katar assist Dan with standing up. He was healed, but they still wanted him to be careful.

I stood and then immediately dropped back to my knees.

"Jolie?" Dan asked, turning towards me.

"Dizzy," I whispered.

"Today was rather eventful," Kara said, setting her hand on my shoulder. She used her magic to check me. "She needs water and rest. Fox, carry your mate."

Fox jogged over and picked me up. "Yes, Mother."

"Nico, teleport back to the house," Kara said. "I'll be over shortly. Get her into bed, or at least on the couch, and give her a glass of water."

"Yes, ma'am," Nico said.

"I'm going to stay here for a bit," Deryn said, coming to kiss me on the cheek. "I'll come home soon."

"Stay safe," I whispered. My eyes widened and I gasped. "What about the others!"

"What?" Deryn asked.

"Andras, Silver, and—"

"They're safe," Rhys said. "They called me."

I exhaled and felt terrible for a moment.

"Don't worry, we won't mention that you forgot about them," Fox whispered.

"You better not!" I yelled.

"Easy," Rhys whispered, resting a hand on my arm. "Don't get so worked up."

I muttered under my breath, but didn't say anything else. Nico teleported us back to the house, into the living room.

Andras, Silverowl, and Mawrth sat in the living room drinking beers and eating pizza.

"Jolie!" Andras and Silver yelled as soon as they saw us.

"She's alright," Fox assured them. "Just needs to lie down."

"Yes, I'm sure she's had a rough day," Mawrth said with a roll of his eyes.

"Says the pampered prince who can't even win a fight against a pathetic, spoiled girl," I taunted.

"Not today," Rhys growled. "You're not shifting or fighting today."

I glared at him.

"I mean it," Rhys said and turned to face Mawrth. "Stop acting like a brat. You realize that if you fight her, I get to whip your ass afterwards, right? Doesn't matter if she wins or not. She's my mate, and I can fight you afterwards."

Mawrth's face paled a bit. "Whatever. I never said I was going to fight her."

"Pansy," I mumbled.

Fox set me on the couch with a sigh. "Stop."

"He is an ass," I said, pointing at Mawrth.

"And no one is denying that or contradicting you," Andras said. "But, for today you need to calm down and ignore him."

"Why do you always defend her? Did you fall in love with her? Or did she use her siren's ability to lure you in?" Mawrth asked.

Andras snapped, his body becoming covered in scales as he slammed Mawrth to the ground. "She isn't my mate, but she is my brother's, which means she is family. She is also carrying my future niece or nephew. Even Mother has let go of her issues, and has welcomed Jolie. Why can't you?"

Mawrth glared at Andras, but no matter how hard he struggled, he couldn't free himself. Andras was stronger, and clearly more powerful, since I knew not many dragons could hold the form he was currently in.

"I'm going to check on Deryn," Nico said, kissed my cheek, and then teleported away.

"Nico?" a somewhat familiar voice called from the front room.

Andras, Rhys, and Silver disappeared from the room.

Fox picked me back up, and held me against his chest. Mawrth stood, brushing off his clothes.

The next second, Nico's brother Klaus appeared beside me. "My, your mates are awfully rude. I just came to see my brother, and—"

He stopped talking, and focused on my stomach, which was odd since I was in Fox's arms and I wasn't big enough to tell from just a look yet. How did he know?

"Klaus, Nico isn't here," I said.

"You know him?" Rhys asked as everyone reentered the room.

"He is one of Nico's half-brothers," I explained.

"You're pregnant," Klaus whispered.

"What?" I asked.

He reached out towards me, but Fox stepped away from him, curling his body around mine protectively.

"You've got a little bundle of magic in your belly," Klaus said. "I sense a bit of it being a mage, but there's other magic, too."

"It's a hybrid," I answered. "And, don't ask. The answer is strange and complicated."

"Nico's?" Klaus asked.

I nodded, since he was one of the fathers.

Klaus's eyes darkened, and he turned to face Rhys. "You're the dragon mate, yes?"

Rhys nodded.

"You and I need to speak in a room away from her," Klaus said. He turned and smiled at me. "No offense, sister, but your heartbeat is erratic and I don't want to get you anymore stressed."

Sister?

Rhys, Andras, and Klaus walked out of the room.

"Stay on the couch," Fox ordered me as he set me down.

"Okay," I agreed, laying down on the couch, and getting comfortable.

"I'm getting her water," Fox said. He looked at Silver. "Don't let her get up."

Silver smiled and sat on the end of the couch where my feet were. He picked them up, set them in his lap, and started massaging them.

I moaned, and stayed very still as he massaged them.

"She's not going anywhere," Silver assured him.

Fox nodded and then left the room.

"Is Dan alright?" Thor asked as he rejoined us.

Dear goddess! I'd completely forgotten about Leona, who had teleported with us, and Thor, who had been here!

"Yes," Leona answered. "Kara healed him in time."

I closed my eyes and looked away from them to hide my feelings. How had I ignored Leona? How had I forgotten she was there? She was my best friend.

"Jojo, what's wrong?" Leona asked as she knelt beside me.

"Nothing," I lied.

"Jojo," she said in reprimand.

"Later," I whispered. "When we're alone."

"Okay," she agreed, kissed my cheek, and then left with Thor.

I exhaled, and rubbed a hand down my face.

Silver found a particularly sore spot, and rubbed with his knuckle.

I gasped, and wiggled my toes as he worked the knot loose.

"Does no one rub your feet?" Silver asked.

I opened my eyes and knew I was blushing. "Not often."

Fox had returned, and held out a water glass to me.

"She never asks for it," Fox said.

"She's pregnant. Pregnant women get a lot of swelling in their feet and ankles," Silver said. "You should rub her feet, the tops of them, and her ankles and shins."

"Noted," Fox said with a nod.

"How do you know about that?" I asked Silver.

"I've helped Mother with a lot of deliveries," he said nonchalantly.

"You're going to make some woman very happy," I said.

He blushed and turned his face away from me.

"Here," Rhys said, handing me a plate of several types of cut up fruits.

"Thanks," I whispered, set the plate on my lap, and began eating pieces.

"Can I go home now?" Mawrth asked.

"Yeah," Rhys said with a sigh. "Thanks for helping earlier."

Mawrth gave me a glare and then headed towards the stairs.

"I'm going to fight him," I told Rhys with a growl before shoving a piece of a pear into my mouth, glaring at the opening Mawrth had walked through.

Rhys sighed. "It won't fix anything. I don't know what you're going to do, but something will happen to change his mind, and it won't be you defeating him."

"A few hits to the head wouldn't hurt anything," I grumbled.

"She's not wrong," Andras muttered.

"Don't encourage her," Rhys said with a sigh. "Just, drop it for now."

"What did my brother-in-law have to say to you?" I asked, looking at Rhys.

"Nothing important," Rhys lied.

I snorted, shoved another piece of pear in my mouth, and then said, "You're a terrible liar."

"Can we turn a show on?" Fox asked, heading to get the remote.

"Yes!" I shouted, mouth still full of fruit.

Fox started a drama we'd recently started watching and sat on the floor in front of me.

Nico and Deryn returned shortly thereafter, but Rhys pulled them away before I could say anything to them.

I wanted to go confront them, but I'd promised to stay on the couch. So, I stayed. I finished off the fruit, set the plate on the floor beside Fox, and lay on my side, curling my legs up a bit.

CHAPTER 17

RHYS

"What are you doing here?" Nico demanded of Klaus.

I'd grabbed Nico and Deryn as soon as they had returned to come talk to Klaus. I could have just given them the message, but I thought it better for Klaus to deliver it himself.

"I came to warn you," Klaus said. "I spoke to our brother and—"

"Which one?" Nico asked. His face was drawn and he looked exhausted.

"What did you call him? Trident Douche?" Klaus asked with a smirk.

"Where is he?" Nico asked, his eyes glowing and sparks crackling around his hands.

Oh, boy. He was close to losing control.

"Nico," I warned.

He exhaled, and relaxed.

"He is preparing for war," Klaus said, the smirk gone. "He means to kill you, your mate, and as many of your kind as possible." He looked at me. "Yours." He looked at Deryn. "And yours, too."

"What do you know?" I asked. "What else can you tell us?"

"He will wage war at each of your homes, but won't contain it to those spots. He means to wreak havoc, and start a panic as far as possible," Klaus said.

"What type of army does he have that he thinks he can defeat us with?" Nico asked.

"I'm not sure. He was just raving like a lunatic about killing you all and torturing your mate before killing her," he said and shook his head sadly.

"We won't let that happen," I growled, and Deryn growled as well.

"Thank you, for telling me," Nico said. "I appreciate the warning."

"I can't help you," Klaus said softly. Even I could see the war within his eyes. "I won't come between siblings."

Nico nodded. "It's alright, Klaus. I understand. If the tables were turned, I wouldn't want to come between siblings, either."

Klaus smiled and glanced at the door. "Keep her safe. There's something special about that girl."

"We know," Nico said, smiling. "We'll protect her at all costs."

Klaus nodded once more and then teleported out.

"How's everything at the werewolf den?" I asked, looking at Deryn.

"Good. Dad's already walking around, preparing everyone for a possible next attack," Deryn said. He sighed. "I still can't believe they hurt him so badly."

"We need to up our training," I said.

The other two nodded.

"We should get back out there, or she's going to come looking for us," I warned.

"This war isn't going to end well for Jinla," Nico whispered. "If he uses his siren powers—"

"We've got Leona and Jolie," I reminded him. "Jolie can use her siren powers even from here."

"She's not trained well enough yet," Deryn argued.

"I have faith that our mate can cause wide-spread panic from her bed with just the twitch of her finger," I joked.

"Your words are too possible for my liking," Nico grumbled.

"I'll talk with Leona about focusing her training to be an asset against Trident Douche and his armies," I promised.

We returned to the living room, and all ignored Jolie's glare. I just hoped this war wouldn't start until after our child was born. Once our child was born, we would triple the guards, and kill anyone who entered our territory without permission. No one was going to hurt them. No one.

CHAPTER 18

JOLIE

"I thought I wasn't supposed to be using my powers or stressing myself while pregnant?" I asked Leona.

She stood across the grass from me, stretching her arms above her head.

"I've been asked to up your training and get you in fighting shape. Well, siren fighting shape anyway," she said, smiling wide.

"What type of torture must I endure today?" I asked, sighing in resignation. I knew they wanted me to be strong so I could protect myself. And, I wanted that, too.

"I'm going to teach you to cause anger," she said.

"What?"

"I'm going to teach you how to make others angry. It's something I'm sure you'll be great at," she said with a wide smile.

"I don't know if that's a compliment or not, but I've been trying it and haven't been able to. I hope you've got a trick up your sleeve," I said, returning her smile.

"Sit and close your eyes. This is going to be an emotional ride."

I obeyed.

"Focus on Deryn. You should be able to focus on him through your mate bond," she explained.

I opened my bond with Deryn more than it already was, narrowing my bonds with the others, to focus on him. "Okay," I whispered.

"Think of something that really pisses you off. Something that makes you want to tear people's heads off," she said.

That was easy. I thought about internet lag causing me to lose my connection to the *Ghost 2* servers, and causing the team to wipe during the last step of the hard raid boss's fight. That bastard had had only a tick of health left. All we had to do was hit him once, and we would have won. Unfortunately, I was the last one alive, and right when I was about to hit him, my internet gave out, wiping us, and making us start over.

The anger built in me.

"Channel that anger to Deryn. Think of it like pushing the feeling down your mate bond," she said.

I imagined the anger as a red aura, and slid that red glow down our bond, coating it, and sending a wave at Deryn.

We heard a roar inside, and something shattered.

My eyes flew open, and Deryn marched outside, eyes glowing. "What are you doing?" he demanded. His hands were bleeding.

I started to stand, but Leona put a hand on my shoulder. "She's working on her powers."

"Warn me next time," he growled.

"What happened to your hands?"

"I was holding a glass vase, and suddenly, got so mad that I just smashed it in my hands," he said. He started to pick out the pieces of glass, not even wincing.

"Sorry," Leona said, wincing for Deryn.

"She did it though, right?" he asked.

Nico teleported to us. "I've got an idea."

"Okay," Leona said.

"I'm going to bring the others out, and we are going to spar. I want you to randomly send emotions to us," Nico said. "I want to see how it effects our fighting."

Leona nodded. "Then, I want you to send one emotion to all of them at once. So, we can see how effective it is when you send to multiple people."

"Got it," I said, and shifted my butt on the ground to get a bit more comfortable. Our grass was incredibly soft and lush, though. So, I didn't have to shift much.

"Let us change, and then we'll be out," Nico said.

"Food?" I requested.

He smirked, bent to kiss my lips, and whispered, "As my queen orders."

I sat still, trying my best to meditate before my next attempt.

The guys returned, and Leona whispered, "Do not open your eyes."

"Why not?" I asked, but obeyed.

"Just, don't," she said.

"Is it bad?"

She sighed. "Are we friends?"

"Duh," I said with a closed eyes eye roll.

"Then keep your eyes shut, and don't open them until we finish this test," she ordered me.

"Fine," I grumbled, wondering what she saw that she thought might hinder my ability to focus.

"Ready," Deryn called from somewhere behind me.

"Begin sparring," Leona instructed them. "Then, I'll instruct her to start.

Leona sat next to me, leaning her shoulder against mine, but facing the opposite direction as me. I assumed she was facing the guys, but I didn't bother asking.

I could hear the guys sparring behind me, their feet shuffled along the grass, and there were smacks of flesh against flesh.

"Enrage Fox," she whispered.

I opened Fox's bond, remembered the game killing me for no reason, telling me I was killed by the "architects", and wiping the team. Anger built in me, and I sent the red aura down Fox's bond.

Instantly, Fox snarled, and the movements behind me increased.

"Enrage Deryn," she said, her voice just loud enough for me to hear.

I repeated the steps, but kept Fox's link open and some of the anger sliding down his bond as well.

Deryn growled, and the fighting intensified behind me.

"Now, all of them," she said. "At the same time. I want you to pull all of the anger back, form it into a tight ball of rage, and then send it down all four bonds at once."

I gritted my teeth, opened all four bonds, drew the anger back from Deryn and Fox, and built the anger up until the red ball almost filled me up. Then, I sent it down all four links.

All four roared, and I heard Deryn shift and Rhys shift as well. Then, I felt the ground moving, and fire behind me.

"Holy shit!" Deryn roared.

"This is amazing!" Fox screamed.

"Turn around," she said, "but keep those bonds filled with rage."

I opened my eyes, and turned, looking at my four mates in their most dangerous forms, fighting each other.

Damn, they were gorgeous. They wore only sweatpants, and their bodies were covered in sweat as they fought each other.

"Close your eyes, draw it all back, then send them all the love you can," she instructed me.

"Love?" I asked.

She nodded.

I closed my eyes, and obeyed. I drew the red back into me, and let it drown in a ball of silver. I thought of how much I loved them, and how happy they made me.

When I opened my eyes, the guys stood perfectly still, looking at me with tears in their eyes.

"Girl, that is amazing," Leona whispered.

The guys came to me, dropped to their knees, and took turns hugging me.

"We love you, too," Nico whispered in my ear.

"Well, it looks like that was a success," Andras said behind me.

"Ah, just who I wanted to find," Leona said.

I pulled away from Nico to look at Andras and Leona.

Andras arched a brow. "Me?"

She nodded, an evil smirk on her face. "I need you to spar with Rhys."

Andras walked to the spot they used for sparring, tossed his shirt to the ground, and took a fighting stance. "Ready."

"Damn, that is one fine male," Leona whispered.

"You're dating Thor," Fox whispered with a chuckle.

"I can appreciate the way another male looks. I just can't touch," She said. She looked at me. "Right?"

I raised my hands. "I'm not touching that conversation with a ten-foot pole."

"Traitor," she muttered.

Rhys walked to Andras, stood a few feet away, and took a fighting stance. "Ready," he called out to me.

"Use your bond with Rhys, and then the dragon's bond to find Andras," she instructed me.

"Shouldn't she rest first?" Fox asked, folding his legs beneath him next to me.

"No. I need to see what she can do," Leona said.

"Okay," I agreed.

I closed my eyes, and focused. I opened Rhys's bond, and then used our bond to travel down the dragon's bond to Andras. I found him, easily enough. "Got him."

"On my mark, send the fury to Rhys, and then to Andras," she said.

I nodded to let her know I understood.

"Start sparring," Leona called out to Rhys and Andras.

They began.

"Focus on Andras," Leona whispered. "Don't let it go anywhere else."

Right.

"Now," she whispered.

I obeyed and heard Andras roar and shift.

"Holy crap," Rhys said. "You shifted into warrior form."

Andras responded by roaring, and continuing his attack.

"Draw it back," Leona whispered.

I obeyed, but couldn't get all of it. "I can't get it all," I choked.

"Calm down," she whispered, and a cool wind wrapped around me, easing my worry. "Try again."

I took a deep breath, and then imagined breathing in all of the red anger. Slowly, it pulled away from Andras, and back into me, where I smothered it with love again, but this time, I didn't send that out to Andras.

I heard Andras gasping, and opened my eyes to find him laying on the ground on his back with Rhys beside him.

"Is he alright?" I asked. "Are you alright?" I called to Andras.

Andras raised a hand with one thumb up.

I exhaled in relief and sagged against Leona's side. "No more," I begged. "I'm exhausted."

"That was amazing!" Andras roared, fists raised.

"He's never been able to take a warrior form before," Rhys said as they walked towards us.

"How many people could she do that to?" Andras asked.

"I'm not sure," Leona admitted. "Or how long she could hold it for."

"How does anger affect the elves?" I asked Fox.

"Similar to the others, but we don't have a form to shift into. Your rage did give me an extra boost of my earth affinity, though."

"I thought I'd felt the ground rumbling," I said. I lay on my back, and took several deep breaths.

"This is good," Nico said with a nod. "This is very good."

"Water," I requested.

Nico teleported away, and then returned the next moment with a bottle of water.

I drank it all in three gulps, gasping for breath when I was done, and wiped at the water that had dribbled down my chin.

"No more for today," Nico said, picked me up, and teleported me to our room.

"I'm fine," I assured him. "I'm just tired."

"Which is why I'm putting you in bed," he said. "The guys and I have some planning to do, and this will alter our original plan a bit. So, you rest here, while we discuss our strategy."

"I don't like that you plan things without me," I told him, but as I lay on the soft bed with the warm blanket now settled on me, I was having trouble keeping my eyes open.

"Rest, and when you wake up, I'll explain our plan to you. Okay?" He kissed my forehead, and teleported away before I could respond.

"Fine," I grumbled, but even though I wanted to argue, I was tired, and a nap sounded amazing.

CHAPTER 19

FOX

"How many are we going to leave to protect her? And which of us? I'm not leaving her without one of us here," I said as we stood over the map of Jinla in Deryn's office.

We had left Jolie to nap, so we could strategize and figure out our plan a, b, c, and d. Just in case. Since things involving our mate often went awry. Not usually because it was her fault, but still, it was better to be prepared.

"Who wants to stay behind?" Rhys asked.

No one spoke up. While we all wanted Jolie protected, we also wanted to be on the front lines, to kill the punk who had tried to erase our mate's memory.

"I'll stay," I said with a sigh. "You all are more powerful and needed on the front lines."

"You sure?" Rhys asked.

I nodded. "Yeah. Just give him a few extra hits from me."

Deryn bared his teeth. "You got it."

"Alright. So, we'll leave Fox, Andras, Martin, Sharla, and Silverowl here," Rhys said.

We all nodded.

"Thor and Leona will be coming with us," Rhys continued. "We need Leona on the front lines in case Douche shows up and starts using his siren powers. Nico, I'll put you in charge of them, so you can teleport them to wherever they're needed when he shows up."

Nico nodded. "Understood."

"Deryn, you and the wolves will need to split up. I want a few wolves on each corner of the city," Rhys said. He put a few metal pieces around the map of Jinla. "I also want five wolves at the den to protect the kids, and those unable to fight."

"We've got the group for that picked out already," Deryn said with a nod.

"Fox, have you decided your defenses yet?" Rhys asked.

"Most of our forces are going to the center of the city. We want to be there, ready to be dispatched where necessary. Our healers are going to be stationed here, here, and here," I said and put markers down on the map. "That way they are centralized and able to heal anyone who needs it."

"Three guards on each healer," Rhys said.

"One mage will be with each healer," Nico said, and put markers next to the ones I'd placed.

"I've changed my mind," Klaus said as he teleported into the room.

Rhys stopped his fist an inch away from Klaus's face, snarling. "Stop doing that!" Rhys growled.

"What did you change your mind to?" Nico asked.

"I can't let Jolie or the baby get hurt," Klaus said, scowling. "He wants to hurt them to get at you, but they're too precious to be killed."

"We don't know you. We can't trust you," Rhys said.

"That baby is the first hybrid in over two hundred years," Klaus said, folding his arms across his chest. "Jolie is unifying our clans, and so quickly that it's blowing the old males' minds. They have no way to combat it. She's unifying not just our clans, but the humans with us. Something not possible before. I will protect her. I will keep her and the baby alive. May I lose my magic, and life, if I fail."

He was being serious. He was telling the truth.

"I think we should let him stay with Jolie," I said, meeting Klaus's eyes. "If he betrays us, he knows we'll kill him."

Klaus smiled. "Exactly. And what idiot wants to anger the four princes?"

"Your brother," I reminded him.

He rolled his eyes. "That's because he's always been stupid and full of anger. He thinks this is revenge for not being able to take the siren throne."

"Fine," Rhys agreed with a slight snarl. "You stay and protect Jolie."

"How are we going to contact each other when this starts?" Klaus asked. "This could happen at any moment."

"Day Star," Nico said.

Day Star was a mage spell that sent a huge ball of light in the sky that flashed bright enough to blind you if you looked at it directly. The flash could be seen for hundreds of miles. It was the easiest way to send a signal to everyone. Most high-level mages could perform the spell, so no matter who saw the first attack, everyone would know it had started.

Klaus nodded.

"I have an idea," Leona said from the doorway.

We all spun, eyes wide since none of us had heard her approach.

"Sorry," she said and smirked. "Didn't mean to frighten you boys."

"What is it?" Rhys asked.

145

She set two silver cylinders on the table. They were small, and looked familiar.

"These are earplugs," she said.

"We can't be deaf while being attacked," I said.

She rolled her eyes at me. "I swear, you guys act like women are stupid sometimes and it's just so barbaric. I see why Jolie gets so worked up when discussing battles with you."

"We don't—" Deryn started, but she waved his words away.

"Look. These are magic ear plugs. They're designed to make you deaf to a siren's call. So, no matter what Trident Douche tries to sing, you won't be affected," she explained.

"What about Jolie's powers?" I asked.

She smiled, joy and pride shining in her eyes. "My girl can still use her powers on you because she's doing it through the bond, not through sound."

Well, that was good to know. Also, slightly terrifying.

"Martin and Sharla will be moving in tomorrow," Rhys told us.

"You didn't tell Jolie that," Leona said, eyes wide.

"No, we didn't," Nico said and sighed. "We had planned to, but forgot today."

"She's going to be mad," Leona said in a sing-song voice.

"We need Sharla here in case she goes into labor and Kara is unavailable," Nico explained.

"And, having Martin here to protect her doesn't hurt either. Since, we all know he still loves her even if it's no longer romantic," she said.

We all cringed slightly. He did still care for her. He loved his mate, but part of him still belonged to Jolie. Just like if she hadn't taken us as mates, we still would have belonged to her.

"He offered. Plus, we will have several powerful guards here, which makes his mate and daughters safer than just at the werewolf den," Deryn said.

She smiled. "Don't try to convince me, wolfie boy. It's your mate that you have to deal with."

"She'll understand," I said, confident.

"Of course, I will," Jolie said, leaning her shoulder against the doorjamb. "Although, I would rather be told things *before* they are decided on."

"You're supposed to be sleeping," Nico grumbled.

"I slept for thirty minutes and then couldn't stay asleep because *someone* decided to take up martial arts in my stomach," she explained, and glanced down.

We all looked at her stomach and saw the baby pressing against her skin from the inside, the perfect outline of a baby's foot visible through her skin. The foot disappeared, and her entire belly seemed to shift around as it moved. Damn, it was moving around a lot, and was considerably larger.

Deryn was closest, so he bent a sniffed. "Dragon."

Rhys walked over, knelt, and pressed his forehead to her belly.

The baby kicked him in the forehead.

I let out a bark of laughter and then clamped a hand over my mouth. "Sorry," I mumbled.

Deryn smirked but had kept his laughter in somehow.

Rhys growled, and the baby instantly stilled.

"Don't scare the baby!" Jolie snapped, backing away from him and putting her hand to her stomach. The baby kicked her hand, and she scowled. "Fine, scare away."

"I'm not scaring the baby," Rhys said, pulling her by the hand so she came back closer to him. "It's a dominance thing. Our child is an alpha, and we only understand one thing, dominance."

"Because you're all so pigheaded and stubborn?" Jolie muttered beneath her breath.

"Yes," I agreed.

She looked up at me and smiled.

There it was. The most beautiful smile in the world. She

glowed, radiating strength and beauty in her pregnancy. I was one lucky male.

"Child, we need you to calm down, so we can talk out how best to protect you and your mother," Rhys whispered. "Understand?"

The baby leaned into his forehead, and stilled.

Jolie's eyes filled with tears, but she quickly wiped them away, and turned on us with hands on her hips. "Fill me in." She looked around the room, and her eyes widened when she saw Klaus. "Klaus? What are you doing here?"

"He's decided to assist us after all," Nico explained.

Klaus smiled. "I've come to assist with guarding you," he explained and then looked at her stomach. "And your child."

"Thank you," she said. She came the rest of the way into the room, stopping on my right, and looked at the map. She scowled a moment, and pointed at the location of the new school she had created. "What about the school? What happens if they're attacked?" she asked.

We all looked at each other. We hadn't really thought about that.

"I'll have a few wolves go to guard it and the kids, but I don't think they'd stoop so low as to attack children," Rhys said.

"They're not really kids," she said. "They're teenagers. I would consider Gavin a threat, and they should as well. They may be young, but they can still do plenty of damage."

She wasn't wrong. Gavin may not have been as strong as Rhys or Andras, but he could kill plenty of humans and his fire would destroy vampires easily enough.

"Plus," she continued. "What better way to hurt people than to kill their children."

We all tensed at that, because she was right.

"Okay," Rhys said. "I'll get a few to protect them."

She nodded, and resumed looking at the map. "You think he'll attack Atlantis?"

"I doubt it," I told her. "He would have to get his armies to Atlantis first. Not even Nico can teleport there."

"It's warded," she said. "That's why." She was silent a moment and then snarled. "If they hurt Pookie, I'm going to tear their arms off."

"Pookie?" Klaus asked.

"Her pet kraken," I answered.

His eyes widened, and he looked at her with awe. Yeah, she was pretty awe-inspiring.

"I'm sure they won't hurt Pookie," I assured her. If they were smart, they would stay away from her pet. I didn't want to see the rage she'd unleash if they killed Pookie.

"They better," she growled, her eyes glowing a moment, but then reverting to normal as she resumed looking at the map.

"So, who is babysitting me?" she asked. "Aside from Martin, Sharla, and Klaus?"

"Andras, Silverowl, and me," I answered.

She looked at me with wide eyes. "You're staying behind?"

I shrugged. "The others will be more instrumental out there."

"And, you don't want to leave me without at least one of you here," she guessed, nodding. She took a step to the side, so our hips touched, and then leaned her head on my shoulder. I wrapped my arm around her, pulling her tightly against me. Touching her completed the bond, and everything felt perfect.

"You're still tired," Nico accused.

She glared at him, a glare that could frighten even alphas. "I told you, the baby woke me up. And, I'm *always* tired now."

"Jolie—" Rhys started, but she turned her glare on him.

"I'm not leaving," she said, finality in her words.

She could order us to do just about anything as our queen, and we would have to do it. Yet, she rarely chose to order us around. Normally, she gave us suggestions or asked us to do something to avoid the orders being backed with magic. It was extremely considerate, and we all appreciated it.

Nico disappeared, and then reappeared behind me with the love seat. "Sit," he ordered her.

She glared at him, but huffed and sat. I felt cold without her against my side, but shoved those feelings aside.

Leona sat next to Jolie, and started petting Jolie's hair. Jolie leaned into Leona, and her entire body relaxed.

Leona coming to live with us had worried me initially, but having a girlfriend here turned out to be just what Jolie needed. She needed another female she had a bond with that she could relax and vent to.

I would have preferred to fill that role, but I was happy with our current situation.

"What happens if they focus the attack?" Deryn asked Rhys.

Rhys sighed. "This is where it gets frustrating. Where would they focus an attack? Our house? Or the elves or dragons, since they already attacked the mages and the werewolves? Or simply the city to cause chaos?"

"I hope they start with us," I said, smiling. I was more than ready to crack that Trident Douche's head open. I had never hated anyone, but Justina had been the first, followed quickly by Trident Douche.

"It's hot when Fox is angry," Jolie whispered to Leona.

"I can hear you," I reminded her, turning to give her a smile.

She smiled back. "I know. Turn around. I was enjoying the view."

I obeyed and then flexed my buttock muscles a few times, which made her burst into a fit of giggles.

"Fox," Rhys growled.

I wiped the smile from my face. "Right, sorry. Serious, Fox."

CHAPTER 20

LEONA

I hadn't been too sure about these four males when I first met them. Jolie was special, much more special than any of them knew. She deserved to be worshipped, and surprisingly enough, these males seemed to worship her.

Well, not truly, but they genuinely loved her and would lay down their lives for hers, so it was enough.

And, they were pretty good guys.

I walked in my room and screeched. A huge frog sat on my bed. It made a ribbit sound, jumped off, and moved towards me. Only one person would pull a prank like this.

"Nico!" I screamed.

I heard him chuckle wherever he was in the house, and then he appeared in my room. "What?" he asked.

I pointed at the huge frog. "Don't 'what' me! Get that disgusting thing out of here!"

"Aw, you're going to hurt his feelings," he accused, as he headed towards the frog.

A week after I had moved in, Nico started pulling pranks on me.

The other guys told me it was his version of hazing. They said it would eventually taper off, but not soon enough for my liking.

"Sorry," he mumbled. "I couldn't resist. I saw it and just knew I'd get that screech out of you."

"Jerk," I mumbled and tore the blanket off my bed. "Now I have to wash this."

He disappeared with the frog, and I sighed.

All in all, it was worth it. There was so much here that we missed out on in Atlantis. I loved Atlantis, but I also really loved video games and movies.

"Another prank?" Deryn asked, leaning his shoulder against my doorjamb.

I nodded. "Big frog."

He smiled. "That means he likes you."

I rolled my eyes. "We're not toddlers."

He moved out of my way, and followed me down to the laundry room. "Where's Thor?"

I shrugged. "Not sure."

"You haven't talked to him today?" he asked, disbelief coloring his tone.

I stopped and sighed. "We had a fight."

"I'm sorry," Deryn said, and he genuinely sounded sorry.

I turned and looked at him. "Why are you werewolves so damn territorial? It's irritating."

He smirked. "What happened?"

"Some guy hit on me while we were at a bar, while he was in the bathroom. I turned him down, nicely, and that made Thor mad," I explained.

Deryn chuckled. "He'll apologize later today. I'd bet money on it."

"We'll see," I said, and resumed walking.

"Don't worry, he won't end your relationship over this," he said, still following me.

"How do you know?" I asked, stopping again to face him, hiking the blanket up higher in my arms.

He smiled. "I know wolves, and while I don't know Thor that well, I do know him a bit. He truly cares for you. He's just feeling hurt that you didn't tell the guy to take a hike. It's a stupid wolf thing. He'll realize he is overreacting and call and apologize."

"So, it's like the time you got all rage monster when you saw Martin hug Jolie?" I asked, smirking.

His eyes turned gold a moment, but it was gone before I could say anything. "Yes," he said. "Exactly like that."

"I hope so," I muttered, and returned to my trip to the laundry room.

"You know, if you love him, you should just tell him," Deryn whispered beside me.

I turned, wide-eyed. "What?"

He shrugged. "Just saying. If you do love him, it would help him calm down if you told him that. Knowing you love him would at least let him know you're not going to end the relationship anytime soon. It's not an agreement to be mates, but it soothes the beast in us so we aren't worried about staking a claim."

"Whatever," I mumbled, and pushed open the laundry door with my foot. I paused, and looked back at him. "Thanks, Deryn."

He smiled. "Anytime. Oh, and dinner will be ready in about an hour."

I let the door close behind me and exhaled. They sure didn't act like princes. But, I was glad for that. Especially, since Jolie definitely didn't act like a princess.

I smirked, remembering all the times we played in the mud, and how mad the guards would be when they took her home and had to explain why she was so filthy.

Eventually, her father stopped making her wear dresses, and just let her be.

Those were some of the best days of my life.

When she disappeared, exiled, it broke my heart. If I hadn't had Colton, I doubted I would have come out quite as sane. Not that I was fully sane, but I definitely would have lost a few more screws without him.

I needed to take a trip and go visit him. I'd have asked Jolie if he could move here, but I doubted the guys would be okay with that. As it was, if I ended up mating with Thor, I wasn't sure if I would be allowed to stay here and have him move in. Or, if I would have to move out with him. I didn't really want to leave Jojo. She needed me. Maybe not forever, but she needed someone who could contain her powers, at least until she mastered them.

Once her child was born, it would be easier to train her. As it was, the child added to her instability.

After we killed the Douche of Atlantis, our lives would improve dramatically.

I wanted to do it. I wanted to be the one who sung him into his grave. To watch his eyes and ears bleed as I punished him for what he had done to Atlantis, to me, and most of all, to Jolie.

CHAPTER 21

JOLIE

"**S**top kicking me so hard," I grumbled at my belly as we drove to the elves' territory so Kara could tell us the gender.

"He or she is just excited," Rhys said and set a hand on my belly.

The baby kicked him three times, and then pushed against my rib cage so hard, that I gasped in pain.

"Shit," Fox whispered, and pressed against the lump near my ribs. "We've got to stop the baby from doing that. It'll end up breaking one of her ribs."

I gasped for breath and closed my eyes. I wasn't sure what was going on in there, but the baby had been extremely active lately.

"I've got this," Leona said, and leaned around from her seat in the front to sing softly to the baby.

I couldn't hear her words, but they were soothing, melodic, and it made us all relax.

"You've got to teach me that," I whispered, a smile on my face.

"Yes, Princess," she said with a teasing wink.

We climbed out of the vehicle, and Nico put a shield around us. I had been surprised when they agreed to go to Kara, instead of making her come to us.

They had kept me prisoner in the house for so long, I didn't even know what date it was anymore.

"There they are," Katar said, opening the door and smiling at us.

"Father," Fox said and hugged him.

"Shoo," Katar said, pushing Fox to the side. "I need to get to my favorite."

Fox's mouth dropped open. "I can hear you, you know?"

Katar hugged me and placed a hand on my stomach. "Hello, Daughter.

I smiled, leaned around him, and stuck my tongue out at Fox.

"Hello, Father," I replied.

"Ready?" he asked.

I exhaled. "As I'll ever be."

Honestly, I was more nervous than I wanted to admit. I didn't care what gender the baby was, but I also had a dozen names to pick from still.

We walked into the house, and Kara had me lay on the examining table. "It's going to be cold," she told me and squirted jelly on my stomach.

I shivered, which made Kara chuckle.

My four mates took up places around me. Fox stood at my head, rubbing my cheek with his thumb while his hand cupped my cheek.

The other three stood on my sides, staring at the screen that would show the ultrasound, and where Kara would be able to tell us if it was a boy or a girl.

Kara smiled at the guys. "Breathe, boys. It'll be okay."

They exhaled as one, apparently having been holding their breaths.

She placed the wand on my stomach, and a weird black and

grey image shown on the screen. She moved it around, looking at the baby, but avoiding the baby's genital area.

"Everything looks good. Nothing is out of place," she said.

She started to move towards its butt, and then it shifted into a wolf pup. She sighed. "Deryn."

Deryn's mouth had dropped open. "Did it? How? What?"

"Son, order your child to switch back," Katar said, though his wide eyes made me believe this wasn't a normal occurrence.

Deryn leaned down and whispered, "Now is not the time to be a pup. Shift."

The baby squirmed a bit.

Deryn growled, his eyes turning into his wolf's eyes. "Shift," he ordered the baby.

The baby popped from wolf to human in a blink.

"Blue rupees!" I gasped.

"That is not normal," Leona whispered. "Right?"

"Definitely not," Deryn said.

Kara moved the wand again, unperturbed by my strange child. "It's a—"

"Boy!" my mother said as she popped into existence.

Kara's mouth snapped shut. "You're such a brat!"

Mother giggled, and then disappeared again.

"I swear, I'm going to figure out a way to make her corporeal just so I can smack her," Kara growled. She turned and smiled at us. "Congratulations. You are having a boy."

The guys were silent, which was worrying me.

Nico set his hand on Deryn, and then they all placed a hand on each other.

"What are you—" I started to ask, but they all blinked out of existence.

"Where did they go?" Leona asked with a scowl.

"To celebrate," Katar said with a smile. He walked to me and set his hand on mine. "Males always want a boy to take on their mantle. They wouldn't have been disappointed with a daughter, but they don't want you to see how much this excites them."

I rolled my eyes, and sighed. "Boys are so weird."

Leona came over and watched as Kara continued looking at the baby. "You're having a baby, Jolie. It's so crazy."

"I know," I whispered. "At least that narrows down the name decision by half."

Kara chuckled. "Still having trouble?"

I nodded. "I can't decide. I like several of them, but none of them feel like they're perfect. You know?"

She nodded. "I understand completely."

"Especially with it being a hybrid. If it had been Fox's then figuring out a name would have been at least a little easier. But I can't incorporate all the races in one name," I said.

"Well, technically the baby will have two names," Katar said.

"What?" I asked.

"The first name and the middle name," he reminded me.

"Oh, right," I said and nodded.

"Can we bond with our little boy before you leave?" Kara asked, already squatting down.

"You may," I said with a nod.

She whispered to the baby then put her head against my stomach and the baby pressed against her.

Katar took his turn and then led me to the living room. Kara brought me a milkshake, and I greedily gulped it down.

"So good," I gasped between gulps.

"Where'd they go?" Fox asked from the other room.

"Living room, dear." Kara called out to him.

They walked into the room and smiled at me.

"Done celebrating?" I asked, raising my eyebrows.

"Yes," Fox said unabashedly and sat beside me. "How's your milkshake?"

"Amazing," I answered and resumed drinking it.

"We should get home," Rhys said. "Martin and his family will be arriving soon."

I wanted to go home to see Martin and Sharla, but I wanted to finish my milkshake. I still had more than half of it left. I didn't want to chug it down without enjoying some of it.

"Take the glass," Kara said when she saw my internal dilemma.

I smiled, stood, and then kissed her cheek. "Thanks, Mother."

"Anytime, Daughter. Just bring it back when you come visit again. Or, remind me if we visit you first," she said and hugged me.

"Okay," I agreed, hugged Katar, and then waited by the door.

"I'm not sure how I feel about a little male Jolie running around," Leona whispered. "Add in those four, and it sounds like you're going to have your hands full for the next eighteen years."

"Don't remind me," I whispered. "I'm stressed enough with the pregnancy. And I'm trying really hard not to think about delivery."

She hugged me. "It'll be fine."

The drive was filled with quiet, excited murmuring from the guys, but I tuned them out as I looked at my hands, clasped in my lap.

How soon would the attack happen? Where was Justina? What was she planning? I wasn't defenseless and could cause some serious damage, but she had that damn knife. Would she attack me? Or would she attack my mates? I didn't like that we were going to be separated. I understood the reasoning, but I still didn't like it.

"Jolie," Nico whispered.

I jerked, shocked to find we had arrived home.

Nico's brows were furrowed. He picked me up before I could protest, and carried me into the house. For once, he walked instead of teleporting, which I found odd, but he was obviously worried, so I let him walk.

He set me on the bed when we arrived in the room, then

stood before me with crossed arms. "What were you thinking about?"

"Justina," I answered immediately.

His arms dropped and he relaxed. "Oh."

"Come here," I requested and scooted back on the bed.

He sat on the bed between my legs, with his back to me.

I rubbed his tense shoulders. "You're too stressed, Nico. You've got a lot on your plate and I'm not helping. I'm sorry. Maybe you should just let the others worry about me."

He chuckled, captured one of my hands, and kissed my palm. "Love, it wouldn't matter if you had ten midwives, a thousand guards, and the kings guarding you. I would still worry. You're my world, and the thought you might be hurt, or worse, is always in the back of my mind."

"How can I help?" I asked. "There has to be some way for you to relax a bit."

He turned and kissed me lightly. "I'm fine. Although, you laying about more would ease some of my worry."

"All I do is sit around," I groaned.

He smirked. "It'll be over soon." He placed his hand on my stomach. "Then, we'll be able to hold our boy."

I climbed off the bed, headed to the nursery, and erased all the girl names. Nico stood behind me, wrapped his arms around my waist, and pulled me back against his chest. We stood like that for a long time. We probably would have continued, but we heard the door open downstairs.

"Let's go greet our guests," he said, slipping his fingers into mine then teleporting us to the foyer.

"Auntie!" Madison and Tamara yelled, and before I could hug them, shifted into their wolf forms and rubbed against my legs.

I squatted down and pet them. "Hello, girls."

Martin pulled me to my feet, scowling. "Don't squat like that. You're going to get stuck on the floor one of these days, unable to stand."

"Was he this crazy when you were pregnant?" I asked Sharla as I leaned around Martin to look at her.

She smiled, nodded, and then shoved him aside to hug me. She rested her hand on my stomach and the baby kicked her hand. She chuckled. "Do you know what gender?"

"Boy," I answered.

Her eyes lit up. "I can't wait to meet him." She opened her mouth again, but I cut her off.

"No, I haven't figured out a name yet," I said. "There's a board in the nursery with the contenders."

She kissed my cheek. "You'll figure it out."

"I hope so," I grumbled.

"Come on," Nico said. "I'll show you to your rooms."

The family followed Nico up the stairs, leaving me alone in the foyer.

"What are you doing by yourself?" Fox asked, walking down the hallway with a bowl of popcorn.

"Uh—"

He scowled. "Come on. You look like you need some comedy in your life."

I snorted. "I've got all the comedy a girl could want here."

"Want to play some games instead?" he asked.

I smiled and nodded vigorously.

He chuckled. "Why did I even ask? I knew the answer."

He held out the bowl of popcorn, and I gratefully grabbed a few pieces, popping them into my mouth immediately.

We walked side by side, and I already felt happier. A nice perk of being with Fox.

We entered the game room and found Deryn laying on the couch, asleep.

Fox pushed me towards him, nodded his head, and then left the room.

Slowly, and quietly, I lay on my side in front of Deryn. He

wrapped his arm around my waist, scooted back to give me more room, and tugged me back.

I lay my head on his bicep, closed my eyes, and relaxed.

"I love you," he whispered.

"I love you, too, Moon Moon."

"You going to nap with me?" he asked.

"I wouldn't be laying here otherwise," I whispered.

He spooned himself around me, kissed the back of my head, and relaxed.

With him wrapped around me, I felt safe and so incredibly warm.

CHAPTER 22

RHYS

"What do you mean he got beaten up?" I asked Dad.

"Exactly that," he said. "Some guy at the school was starting trouble, and Gavin stepped in, but he bit off more than he could chew."

Gavin wasn't as strong as Andras, but he was strong, and smart. How had he been defeated?

"What was the kid?" I asked.

Dad shrugged. "Gavin won't tell me. He just told me to drop it when I showed up to get him from the principal's office."

"I'll talk to him," I said, and headed out of Dad's office.

"Go easy on him," Dad ordered me.

"I know," I called behind me.

Mawrth glared at me a moment then averted his eyes as we passed each other in the hallway. I hoped he would eventually get over his issues with me and Jolie, but I wasn't holding my breath.

I knocked on Gavin's door twice.

He opened it and smiled. "Rhys!"

I hugged him and ruffled his hair. "Hey, little bro. How's it going?"

He shrugged, stepped back to let me in his room, and then shut his door. "Did Dad send you in here?"

"No. I came to talk to you because I wanted to check on you," I said honestly.

He sat in his computer chair, and spun it around in a circle, tucking his legs up on the chair. "I'm fine. I got beat up, but it happens." He shrugged, and looked at me. "You've been beaten up before."

I nodded. "We all battle an enemy or two who turns out to be tougher than we thought."

"He was picking on a human," Gavin explained. "I couldn't let him do that. Jolie started the school so we would get along."

"What was he?" I asked.

"Werewolf," he said.

"Name?" I asked.

Gavin shook his head. "No way. You're going to tell Deryn, Deryn's going to lecture him, and then that guy is going to kick my butt again."

"How did he kick your butt anyway? You're not weak."

Gavin sighed. "The human was close to me. I didn't want to risk injuring her."

Ah, there it was. *Her.* I thought that might be the case.

"She pretty?" I asked with a smirk.

Gavin smirked and spun his chair again. "Beautiful."

"Did she fawn over you after you got beat up?"

His smirk turned into a smile. "Yeah."

I laughed. "Well, at least there was some good to the beating."

"He's going to be expelled from the school," Gavin said. "They told us that if anyone was caught fighting they would get expelled. They almost expelled me, but the surveillance showed he started it, and that I was protecting her."

"What's *her* name?" I asked.

"I don't know," he said and tilted his head to the side. "I forgot to ask."

"Well, you better rectify that tomorrow," I said.

He nodded. "I plan to."

"Well, it looks like you didn't need a pep talk from your older brother after all. Anything you want to talk about while I'm here? I've got about half an hour before I need to be anywhere."

"How's Jolie?" he asked.

He loved Jolie. He'd immediately taken to her, and it warmed my heart to know my little brother was so fond of her. Thankfully, he wasn't hitting on her like Andras did, but I knew better than to think he wasn't attracted to her. He was a teenage boy, after all.

"She's doing well. We found out we're having a boy," I told him, smiling.

"A nephew?" he asked, his eyes lighting up.

I nodded.

"Did you pick out a name yet?" he asked.

"No," I said and shook my head. "Jolie has a list she keeps staring at, hoping one of them sticks."

"I can't wait to play with him," Gavin said, looking up at the ceiling. His smile slipped and he asked, "How do you keep from hurting a human girl?"

I stopped his spinning chair, sat on his bed so we were face to face, and said, "You just have to keep your strength in mind at all times. Now that Jolie is stronger, I don't check myself like I used to. Just imagine you're touching a baby. That way you don't use too much strength."

"Have you ever hurt Jolie on accident?" he asked.

"I burned her once," I admitted.

He cringed.

"You'll figure it out. Just remember, your first girlfriend won't likely be your last. So, don't be afraid to end it and move on if things don't work out."

"Do you have any regrets?" he asked.

I shook my head. "I wouldn't change anything because if I did, it might mean I wouldn't be with Jolie and about to have a child with her."

"Does it bother you that the child is a hybrid?" he asked.

I shook my head again. "No. It's actually pretty awesome. I love knowing that my best friends and my mate are all part of our child."

"He's going to be magnificent," Gavin said smiling wide. "Just like Jolie."

"She is pretty magnificent," I agreed. Then growled. "And mine."

Gavin rolled his eyes, knowing I was just teasing him since my growl wasn't too deep. "Yeah. Yeah."

I stood, clapped him on the shoulder, and said, "Good luck with your human girl. Feel free to text or call me with questions."

He stood, hugged me, and walked me to the door. "Thanks, Rhys."

I entered Dad's office, shut the door, and smiled at him. "He was protecting a human girl."

Dad chuckled. "That's what it looked like on the surveillance video, but he didn't tell me the human was a girl."

"He likes her," I added.

"Not surprising."

"He asked about not hurting a human. You may want to talk to him some about how to control his strength. Maybe give him some training."

Dad nodded. "Thanks, Rhys."

I shrugged. "Just doing my job as the oldest."

"Mawrth still hate you and Jolie?" he asked.

I scoffed. "Yeah."

"You going to do something about it?" he asked with an arched brow.

"After Jolie gives birth, she's going to kick his ass to establish dominance. I'll take it from there."

Dad threw his head back as he laughed. "Oh, I want front row seats to that!"

"I don't understand how he thinks he will be able to beat her, since she beat Mom," I said.

"She didn't defeat me in a fight," Mom said as she entered.

"She can," I assured her.

"Well, I have no desire to fight my pregnant daughter-in-law," she assured me.

"Good, since she's carrying your grandson," I said with a wide smile.

Dad's eyes widened, and Mom squealed. I had never in my life heard my mother squeal.

She threw her arms around me and danced around. "A boy! A little grandson!"

"You're much more excited than I thought you would be," I admitted. "I thought you'd prefer a granddaughter to spoil."

"Boys are much easier. They like getting dirty and fighting. I'm much better at that," she said.

That was definitely true.

"How's Jolie dealing with being on house arrest?" Dad asked.

"I'm stopping by the game store on the way home to get her the two newest games. That should occupy her for a week or two."

"In other words, she's going crazy," Mom said with a smirk.

"She doesn't mind being home. She hates how much we hover," I said and shrugged. "I can't help it. She's pregnant with my child. I don't want to let her out of my sight, but I'm trying to work on that. That's part of why I'm here. I left her napping on the couch with Deryn."

"She needs as much sleep as she can get," Mom said. "Once the baby is born, she'll get very little sleep."

"Well, she has four mates to help with the baby instead of one, so it shouldn't be too bad," Dad said.

"True," Mom agreed.

"When are you coming over next?" I asked them. I'd rather be prepared than have them show up out of the blue.

"Tomorrow," Mom said. "I want to bond more now that I know the baby is a boy."

I nodded, kissed her cheek, hugged Dad, and then left the house.

At the gaming store, the female cashier couldn't keep her eyes off of me. I'd thought having the mating crystal would be more of a deterrent, but nothing had changed. I avoided eye contact, grabbing the games I knew Jolie would want to play.

"These two games are pretty fun," the cashier said with a smile as she rang them up.

"I hope so. My mate is going crazy at home without some new games," I said.

"Jolie, right?" she asked.

I nodded. So, she did know who I was.

"You should get this, too," she said, and pointed at another new game I hadn't even known was out, *Ghost 3.*

"Oh, she definitely needs that," I agreed.

"I saw her at the tournament," she told me. "She's pretty good."

I smiled, proud of my little gamer. "Yeah, she is."

"Well, I hope she has fun with these. Take care," she said, smiling as I walked away.

I exited the shop and scowled. Had I been wrong? Was she not checking me out?

I turned back and caught her looking at my butt.

My smile returned. Nope. I still had it!

CHAPTER 23

JOLIE

I yawned and stretched out flat on my back, smacking Deryn in the face as I did and almost falling off the couch. Only his strong arm kept me from falling.

"Sorry," I gasped, rolled on my side, facing Deryn, and kissed his face several times in apology.

"You can hit me more often if I get that type of apology," he grumbled, still half asleep.

Chuckling, I kissed his lips. "I'd rather not hurt you and just give you kisses."

"Mm, kisses."

He opened his eyes, smiled, and said, "You're so damn beautiful."

I smirked. "Thank you."

He tried to tug me into him, but my protruding belly kept me from getting any closer. He sighed. "Soon, that baby will be out of you, and I'm going to have my way with you."

"You know we can have sex while I'm pregnant, right?" I asked, arching an eyebrow.

He shook his head. "It's not the same for us. Sensing the baby makes having sex weird."

That explained a lot.

"I see," I said.

He kissed the tip of my nose. "Trust me, you're not the only one going through withdrawals."

I didn't respond, just laid my head back down on his bicep, and closed my eyes.

"Jolie," Rhys called in a sing song voice. "I have presents."

I bolted upright and then groaned as the baby flipped around in my stomach. "Too fast."

Deryn sat up, placed his hand on my stomach, and the baby settled.

"Sorry," Rhys said.

"What did you get me?" I asked with a wide smile.

He held out a bag from *GameStart*, the local video game store. "New games."

I screeched, grabbed the bag, pulled out the games, and then my mouth dropped open.

"No way! They released *Ghost 3*? I didn't even know it was in production," Deryn said.

I leapt up and hugged Rhys, then gave him a long, deep kiss with lots of tongue. "You're the best. I love you."

"Kiss ass," Deryn grumbled.

"Which do you want to play first?" Rhys asked, grabbing the games from me and beginning to take the annoying plastic wrap off of them. I always had problems getting the plastic off, so he did it for me.

"You choose," I said and grabbed a game controller.

"Really?" he asked, looking up at me.

I nodded. "I can't choose between them. I know you guys all wanted to play these, too. So, you choose which one we are going to play first."

"We're going to play together?" Deryn asked.

I smirked. "Well, we all live in the same house. It makes sense for us to sit together and play the game with one another. Unless you guys want to play on your own, so you can get all the trophies and stuff on your profiles. I can understand that."

"No, playing together sounds great," Rhys said.

"I'll get Nico and Fox," Deryn said.

"Food!" I yelled. "Please!"

"Yes, my queen!" Deryn called back.

"How was your trip to your parents' house?" I asked Rhys, getting comfortable on the couch.

"Good. Gavin's got a crush on a girl at school," he told me as he popped the disc into the console.

"Oh? A dragon?"

"No, a human," he said, and glanced up at me.

I blinked. "What? You think it's because of me? I'm not human."

"We all thought you were. And yes, I do think it's because of you. I think you showed him that it doesn't matter what race the girl is, as long as she's nice," he said.

"Can we please go by the school one of these days? I want to see how it's going," I begged. I gave him my best puppy dog eyes and pouted a bit.

"What is she asking for?" Nico said. "And what do we have to do to make it happen?"

I smiled, victorious.

"She wants to go to the school," Rhys said.

Nico scowled, then sighed. "Okay. We'll take you."

I blinked in a silent stupor. Nico had agreed? So quickly?

Nico smiled and sat beside me. "You know we'd do anything for you."

"Yeah, but you've been keeping me on lockdown. I didn't think you'd let me leave," I admitted.

"We're trying to keep you here as much as possible, but I know how much the school means to you," he said.

I kissed him. "You're the best."

"I thought I was the best?" Rhys asked and showed Nico the games he'd gotten.

"You know I don't have favorites," I said with a roll of my eyes.

"You guys can't be her favorite, because I am," Ezio said as he took the open seat on my side, and draped his arm around my shoulders.

I leaned into him a minute, and then straightened, not wanting the guys to get jealous or to be too touchy with a male who wasn't my mate. It was hard, because I was a very touchy person. I enjoyed hugging or leaning on someone. But, I knew the guys didn't like when I touched other males too long. So, I was working on it.

"What are we playing?" Fox asked as he walked in, a huge smile on his face.

"*Ghost 3,*" Rhys answered.

Fox sat between my legs, leaning against the couch, and Nico sat in front of Fox, leaning his head back into Fox's lap.

"Play with my hair, Fox," Nico asked in his imitation of a woman's voice.

Fox ran his fingers through Nico's hair. "You should condition more," Fox told him.

Nico scoffed and sat up. "My hair is super soft."

"Not as soft as Fox's," I argued.

Fox stuck his tongue out at Nico.

"You do have favorites," Deryn accused.

"Pointing out that Fox's hair is softer than Nico's is not me picking a favorite," I argued. "That would be like me saying that Fox's ears are pointier and you thinking that makes him my favorite."

"Let's just all remember, I have the nicest ass," Deryn said, smiling broadly.

"I have the nicest chest," Rhys said, flexing his pecs while waggling his eyebrows at me.

"And, I've got the biggest—" Fox started to say, but stopped when Tamara and Madison ran into the room.

"Heart," I ended for him. "Hello, girls."

They were in wolf form still, which I found a bit odd, but didn't comment.

They pawed at Deryn, and he let them climb up into his lap. Deryn began petting them, scratching under their chins, and behind their ears. It was adorable to see him so relaxed with the girls.

"Food!" Fox yelled and leapt up. He looked at me with wide eyes. "We didn't bring you back food."

"Whoops," Deryn said. "Sorry. I knew I forgot something."

"It's okay. I'll just starve to death," I said overdramatically with a whimper.

That earned me three pairs of eye rolls from the mates left in the room. Fox had left to get some food.

I waited for Fox to return before starting the game, so he didn't miss the intro scenes.

While we all munched on food, we watched the intro. Aliens were angry at us for killing their leader. Now, they wanted revenge. It was our job to destroy them, before they destroyed our world.

The actual game started, so I picked up the controller. Then, immediately groaned. "Forced walk," I complained.

The guys groaned, hating when the game forced you to walk instead of allowing you to run or jump.

Finally, the game let me have control, and I headed into battle.

"Right!" Fox yelled.

I spun right, slammed my fist into the alien's face, and then shot him with my shotgun.

"Archers top left," Deryn called out.

Too late, the line rifle shot to the head killed me.

I handed the controller to Fox, and he took a turn trying to get through the battle.

For hours we played, taking turns fighting enemies, calling out warnings to each other. I hadn't played games with my clan in months, but these guys were my true clan.

That was how we needed to work together during the battle against Justina and Trident Douche. We needed to work together as a clan.

The girls fell asleep in Deryn's lap, but he could easily use the game controller by putting his arms around their little furred bodies, so we let them be.

Sharla and Martin came down at one point to collect the girls and take them to bed. Freed from the girls, Deryn got us more food, and we continued with our gaming marathon.

It wasn't until warm bodies pressed against mine that I realized I had fallen asleep at some point and one of them had carried me to bed. I cuddled up against Nico's back, while Deryn spooned himself behind me, and fell into a happy and peaceful sleep.

WHEN ADELAIDE AND EMRYS CAME TO BOND WITH THE BABY, Leona asked Emrys to assist us with a test.

Emrys agreed, and the entire house came outside to watch.

Sitting on the grass, I tried to ignore all of the people around me.

"I would prefer if you didn't ask me to fight him," Rhys said. "If he does go all out, I won't survive long."

Emrys smiled smugly. "Oh, come on. When was the last time you and I sparred? It will be fun."

"What if it's all of you against him?" Leona asked.

She sat beside me, facing the guys. I was facing them, too, but would soon turn away to use my powers for her little experiment.

"Dad?" Rhys asked.

"Me, fight you four?" he asked.

Leona nodded.

Emrys beamed. "Challenge accepted."

Rhys sighed. "Oh, boy."

Rhys and Deryn removed their shirts, tossing them on the grass near me.

"That's a lot of muscle on display," Sharla whispered from my other side. "How is Jolie going to concentrate?"

"I make her turn away," Leona replied.

Sharla chuckled.

"You two are rude," I said. "I'm sitting right here between you."

Sharla patted my head. "We know, Darling."

Madison and Tamara played on the far end of the grass with Martin, all three in wolf form.

I turned around, ready to begin, but a SUV pulled up, making us all stop.

"Who is that?" Rhys asked.

"My dad," Deryn said, and walked towards the SUV. "What's up, old man?" he asked.

Dan stepped out of the SUV and hugged Deryn. Thor stepped out of the driver's seat, and Leona tensed next to me. She and Thor were still not speaking, which worried me.

"What are you all doing out here?" Dan asked.

"We're experimenting with Jolie's powers," Leona answered. "Care to participate?"

"Whoa, we are not fighting both of them," Fox said.

"I'll gladly participate," Dan said, bent, and kissed my cheek. "What do you need me to do?"

"Go spar with Emrys and the boys," Leona said.

Dan cracked his neck from side to side, smiling wide. "Oh, goodie. I haven't sparred in a few months."

"Dad, no shifting," Deryn ordered him.

"Same for you," Rhys said to Emrys.

"It's like they don't trust us," Dan said with a sigh.

"Children," Emrys said and shook his head.

"Alright, you six start sparring. I'll instruct Jolie from there," Leona ordered them.

"What is she going to do?" Emrys asked, and Dan looked over waiting for the answer, too.

Leona smirked. "You'll find out."

I turned around, set my hands in my lap, and closed my eyes.

I could hear them moving around, flesh hitting flesh, but softly, and they even said the occasional teasing remark.

"Enrage Emrys," Leona whispered.

I opened the bond I had with Rhys, traveled down the dragon's bond, and searched out Emrys. He was easy to find, since he was king. I sent the wave of red into him, and he roared behind me.

The sounds of fighting grew more intense.

"Draw it back and give it to Dan," Leona whispered.

I drew it all back in, and sent it to Dan, whose bond was easier to find, since I had a bond with the wolves aside from the mate bond.

Dan roared, and the fighting movements increased.

"Enrage Rhys," she whispered.

"Dan?" I asked.

"Leave him enraged," she instructed.

I exited Dan's bond, leaving the red energy with him, and went to Rhys, sending some at him.

Rhys growled, and Emrys cursed.

"Send it to all of them. All six," Leona ordered me.

I tried to send it all at once, but it was too difficult. So, I sent it individually until all of them were covered in my red energy.

The fighting behind me sounded brutal, and I could smell blood in the air.

"What did she do to them?" Adelaide asked softly.

"Enraged them," Leona explained.

"Leona?" I asked.

"I want to see how long you can sustain it," she said.

"They're bleeding," I whispered.

"Superficial cuts, Daughter. They're fine," Adelaide assured me.

I took deep, slow breaths and kept the red aura covering each of them. The ground started shaking as Fox used his powers.

"Pull it back," Leona said quickly.

I sucked it all back in, in one sharp intake of breath.

I turned and saw all of the guys stagger forward, then drop to sit on the ground, panting, covered in sweat, and bleeding a bit.

"That...that was exhilarating," Emrys gasped.

"That was fun!" Dan boomed, smiling wide.

"What were you going to do with the ground?" I asked Fox.

He glanced at me and smirked. "Use some roots to wrap around them to hold them."

Dan and Emrys exchanged a look, and then smiled.

"So, I..." My words failed to come out of my mouth, my head grew fuzzy, sound disappeared, and I fell onto my back.

Leona's face appeared over mine, her brows furrowed in worry, and her mouth moved, but I couldn't hear anything.

Fox's face appeared, and his hands started glowing as he reached towards me.

A few moments later, sound returned, my head cleared, and I could sit up.

"Whoa," several voices said as several pairs of hands pushed me back down on the ground.

"I'm fine," I whispered, but stayed lying on the ground.

"She just burned up too much magic," Leona explained. "She was just going to faint."

"Fainting isn't good for the baby," Rhys said.

"I'm fine," I assured him.

"What do you think your maximum number of people is?" Leona asked.

I thought about it. "I'm not sure. It depends on how long I have to hold it. It also takes me awhile to send the rage to each of them, because I have to travel down each bond. Dan and the wolves are easier to get to, but my mates are easiest."

"That was some intense power boost," Emrys said. "What happens if she uses it on someone who isn't a king?"

"Andras took on warrior form during it," Rhys answered.

They finally let me sit up, and I found Adelaide staring at me.

"What?" I asked her.

"Does distance matter?" she asked.

"Physical distance?" Leona asked back.

Adelaide nodded.

"No. Since she's using the bonds, the other person can be anywhere in the world," Leona explained.

Adelaide beamed. "You, my dear, may have just ensured our victory."

"How?" Sharla asked.

"When the battle starts, if she can send that rage out to the kings and princes, it won't matter how many of them there are against us. We will use that rage to destroy them all," Adelaide said.

"I wouldn't be able to send it to you for very long," I said.

She turned to Emrys. "How many dhampirs could you have killed during that rage?"

Emrys shrugged. "A hundred? Maybe more."

Dan nodded. "Yeah."

"That's all we would need," Adelaide said.

Leona looked at me and smiled. "That may work. Fox will be with her, so he can heal her if she uses too much magic. And, if we give her a crystal with some extra magic, she can last even longer."

"I'll start storing energy now," Emrys said.

The baby started kicking, but for once it wasn't painful.

I rested my hand on my stomach, smiling as he kicked my hand. "The baby agrees with this plan."

"Let's hope we don't have a battle until after he's born," Rhys grumbled.

We all knew that we rarely got what we wanted though.

CHAPTER 24

RHYS

Jolie's training intensified once Leona and Adelaide hatched their plan to have her enrage us on the battlefield.

I didn't like it. I was too worried she would overextend herself and cause harm to her and the baby.

But, I was outvoted, so I let the topic drop.

The rage boost would be a huge advantage to us when we fought against the enemy. There was no doubt about that.

"Come here," I requested of Jolie when she came back in from one of her trainings.

She plodded over to me, her movements slow due to her ever growing belly and her training. "Hm?" she asked.

I wanted to pick her up, but her belly was so large that picking her up caused her pain now.

"Let's go shower," I told her. "You're covered in sweat, dirt, and grass."

She nodded, and headed towards the stairs, gripping the rail.

I walked a step behind her, ready to catch her if she stumbled, but she made it to our floor without incident. I ushered her into the bathroom while I got a change of clothes for the both of us.

When I returned to the bathroom, clothes in hand, she had started the water, and managed to pull her shirt off, but then sat on the toilet's closed lid.

"Need some help?" I asked.

She glared at me, but nodded.

She didn't like asking for help. She didn't like needing help. My little fighter tried so hard to do things on her own, to keep from being a burden, but thankfully she had learned to accept our help recently. I helped her get the rest of her clothes off.

I stripped, noticing her watching with lust in her eyes. We hadn't slept with her since we found out she was pregnant. It bothered her, but she understood our reasoning. We wanted to sleep with her. We wanted to do a lot of things to her, but our baby was much too aware for us to be able to enjoy doing any of those things while he was inside of her.

I nudged her into the shower, she sighed, and stepped inside. After stepping under the warm water, she started to reach for the shampoo, but I pulled her hand back.

"Let me," I whispered.

"What?" she asked, slightly delirious from fatigue.

"Let me wash you," I said and smiled. "You can barely move and you need a good scrubbing."

"Okay," she said and stepped back.

I lathered up her hair, pushed her a step back into the spray of the water, and rubbed her hair as the soap rinsed out.

Then, I used the bar of soap to wash away the dirt and grass from her skin. She had closed her eyes as soon as I started lathering her hair, and they were still closed as I finished washing her.

"Want to sit in the shower for a bit?" I asked.

Her eyes flew open and she nodded vigorously. She had tried sitting in the shower a week ago, and had been unable to get up, yelling for us to help her stand with flushed cheeks.

I helped her sit down, and then sat on the opposite side of the shower, my feet next to her hips.

She leaned her head back against the tiled wall and closed her eyes. "I miss you," she whispered.

"I'm right here, baby."

She shook her head. "I feel like you're far away. Like we haven't spent much time together. I know we've been together most days, but that's just how I'm feeling. I know it doesn't make sense, but…"

I moved to sit behind her, slipped my arm around her sides, and pulled her head back to rest against my chest. "I'm sorry. I love you."

She sniffled. "Pregnancy hormones suck."

I held in my chuckle, not wanting to upset her because Mother had warned me about this possibility.

"You just tell me what you need, and I'll do it," I promised her.

"This," she whispered, snuggling my arms tighter where they lay just beneath her breasts.

"Would you prefer this in our bed?" I asked.

She shook her head. "I like the warm water."

I sat still, relaxing at the nearness of my mate. She had been through so much, and I feared what lay ahead of us would cause her grief as well. There was always the possibility of casualties in war, and you never knew who would be the one to die.

When she had thought Dan was dying, it had torn her apart. She had been breaking bit by bit until they assured her he would be fine. She hadn't believed them until his stomach had fully healed, though. I'd felt her pain, her sorrow, and knew if she lost Dan or the other kings, she would grieve heavily.

Not having grown up with a true father, she viewed them as fathers now. And, they loved her like a daughter.

Dan and Father had pulled me aside the day we had experimented with her power on them.

"She cannot die during our battle," Father said. "If she does, the battle will be lost."

"Because the four of us won't be able to contain our grief," I agreed with a nod.

Dan shook his head. "No, because you four, and the three of us will not be able to contain our grief. If she dies, the seven of us will fall as well."

I looked down at my mate, the small, adorable gamer girl that she was. She held so much power over kings and princes, and she had no idea. One girl's death would be the death of the city.

That was why she was to be protected at the house. That was why I had spent a few million dollars to hire contractors to add defensive weapons to the house.

I would *not* lose her.

"Rhys," she whispered.

"Yes?"

"We'll have our happily ever after, right? Our lives won't always be like this?"

Her voice was barely more than a whisper, emotions making it crack a bit.

"Yes. We will," I promised her.

She wiped her eyes, sat away from me, and said, "I'm sorry. I—"

I turned her back to face me. "Don't apologize. I want you to tell me how you feel."

"This is pregnancy hormones talking," she said.

"It doesn't matter what is causing it. You can always tell us how you feel," I assured her.

She wasn't used to sharing her emotions and worries with us. It was something we were working on. We knew it wasn't easy for her. Her stepfather had been an abusive jerk, so it made sense that she wasn't used to sharing her feelings.

She leaned against me again, kissed my shoulder, and then rested her head on it. "I love you, Puff."

CHAPTER 25

JOLIE

The guys had finally broken down and agreed to let me go to the city for a group date. Nico didn't come and promised he would make it up to me later, but said he had important king stuff to take care of.

I wasn't the only one who didn't believe him. But, aside from ordering him to come, I couldn't do anything about it.

I walked through a baby store, grabbed a few adorable outfits and stuffed animals, and then stood with the guys at the register to pay.

The clerk's eyes widened when she spotted us. "You're the princess!" she gasped. "I didn't know you were pregnant!"

"We're trying to keep it a secret," I told her.

She eyed my huge stomach. "How?"

Rhys chuckled. "We've been keeping her out of public sight, but she begged us to go out today."

She muttered, "I wouldn't mind being stuck at home with them for a few months."

I suppressed my laugh, and just smiled at her, since I was certain she didn't realize that we could all hear what she had said.

Deryn slipped behind me, pressing his chest into my back, and whispered, "Where are we going next, my queen?"

"Game store!" I said a bit too loudly, getting weird looks from some of the older patrons. I covered my mouth with one of my hands and chuckled. "The game store, please," I said in a normal tone this time.

"Then what?" Fox asked while looking at some pacifiers.

"Food," I said with a wide smile.

"It is almost dinner time," Rhys said after looking at his phone.

The girl held out the bag with our items. "Have a great day, your highnesses."

I waved to her as we walked outside.

All of my happiness disappeared in an instant. The store must have had sound dampeners to keep us from hearing the pure chaos going on outside.

Ogres, trolls, goblins, demons, and dhampirs were attacking the city. Buildings were on fire and people were screaming as they ran for their lives.

"Shit," Deryn growled, moving closer to me.

The guys formed a protective triangle around me.

"The one day Nico takes off would be the day they attack," Rhys growled.

My stomach felt weird, and I felt something move inside my lady parts. I glanced down, like I could see inside. What was going on?

It felt like a balloon had slipped out of me, and then it popped and water filled my pants.

I gasped.

"My water broke!" I all but screeched.

"Shit," Fox said and pulled out his phone.

"We should fly out of here," Rhys said.

A young woman with a toddler screamed to our right as a goblin advanced on them, wielding a sword.

"You need to protect the city," I ordered him. "Fox can drive me home."

"Kara's going to be busy with healing everyone and won't be able to help you give birth," Deryn said.

Fox had been on the phone, but he hung up and said, "I've got it handled. You two help the people."

"You sure?" Deryn asked, looking at me with furrowed brows.

I kissed his lips and whispered, "Protect the people."

He kissed me again, rested his hand on my stomach a moment, and then ran to intercept the goblin.

Rhys snarled, kissed me, touched my stomach, and ran after a troll chasing a group of people down the street.

Fox took my hand. "You've teleported before. Do you think you can do it now?"

I nodded, closed my eyes, pictured home, and used Nico's powers to teleport. When I opened them, we stood in the center of our living room.

A contraction gripped me, and I grunted in pain, bending over slightly.

"Silver!" Fox yelled. "Sharla!"

Silver appeared first. "What?"

"Her water broke," Fox explained. "The city is under attack. The war has begun."

Silver's eyes widened. "Shit. Okay, let's find you a place to give birth. Do you want to try a tub birth or just on a table?"

"Table," I requested.

Sharla stepped into the room. "What's going..." Her eyes dropped to my pants and she rushed forward. "Oh, honey. Your water broke. How long ago?"

"Ten minutes," Fox answered for me.

"Okay," Sharla said softly. "Normally, we still have several hours before the baby comes. So, let's get you comfortable."

"There's going to be a lot of blood," I reminded her. "Where the hell am I supposed to have the baby? I don't want to get blood all over."

Fox was on the phone again, but I didn't pay attention, letting Silver and Sharla lead me to my bathroom.

Silver brought in a cot that had significant padding and was surprisingly comfortable. I lay on it, then grunted as another contraction hit.

"I'm going to grab the supplies," Silver told Sharla. "Stay with her."

Sharla nodded, and sat beside me, holding my hand. "How are you doing, hun?"

"Okay," I said. "It's not too painful, yet."

She smiled. "That's good."

Fox ran into the room. "They're attacking!"

"Go," Sharla snarled. "I've got this."

Martin ushered the girls into the bathroom. "Stay with your mother," he ordered them.

My eyes widened. "Sharla, I don't want them seeing—"

She interrupted me. "They'll stay behind so they won't see anything."

Ezio stood in the doorway, facing the hallway.

"You're on bodyguard duty?" I asked.

He nodded.

Martin kissed his wife and daughters then my cheek, and then left.

Silver returned with a huge bag of supplies, and set it on the bathroom counter. "How're you doing?" he asked.

"Good," I said and then grunted at another contraction.

We all stilled when we heard the sound of rapid gunfire.

"They've breached the wards," Silver said. "That's the turrets shooting."

"Fox?" I asked. "Where's Fox?"

"He's just in the surveillance room," Silver assured me,

pressing on my shoulder to make me lie down again. "Martin is with him and the others are on their way."

I relaxed, but focused on my bonds to see how my other mates were. No one appeared to be injured, which made me relax more.

"Do you want me to bring a TV in?" Sharla asked.

"Is that a good idea?" Ezio asked. "I don't think it's a good idea to get her stressed out during labor."

"I need it so I know when I need to use my powers," I said.

"I'll get it," Silver said. "Sharla, get her changed and check how far along she is?"

Sharla nodded.

Silver left, and then Sharla shut the door so Ezio was outside of it. "Girls, I want you to sit on that bed I made for you," she instructed them. I hadn't seen a bed, but I wasn't really paying too much attention to anything right now.

Sharla helped me strip out of my clothes, and then she put a hospital gown on, and draped a big warm blanket over me. "Alright, spread 'em," she ordered me with a smile.

"This was not how I expected this delivery to go," I grumbled, but spread my legs. "And I did not expect you to be dealing with this."

"Good thing we're friends," she said with a wink. She felt around and her eyes widened. "Shit, you're ready to have him at any moment."

"I don't feel strong contractions yet," I reminded her.

She threw open the door. "Silver! I can already feel his hair!"

I heard Silver cuss, and he ran into the room. "Ezio, set up the TV, please."

My stomach moved to one side as the baby made a sudden movement, and then he began thrashing around.

I yelled in pain, clutching at my stomach.

"We need alphas," Sharla snapped. "Ezio get in here!"

He looked back, wide eyed. "What?"

"She needs an alpha of each race to calm the baby!" Sharla snapped. "Get in here and put your hand on her stomach!"

I yelped as the baby pushed against my ribs, and then he kicked hard, and we all heard the snap just before I screamed.

"Who is nearby?" Silver asked. "Who can we ask?"

Yukio, Declan, and Kylan entered the bathroom.

"What are you three doing here?" I asked, tears rolling down my face.

"Fox called us. Said you would need alphas in case the baby started acting up," Kylan said.

The three came to me. Kylan sat at my head, stroking my hair softly. Yukio and Declan sat on my sides, setting their hands on my stomach where Ezio wasn't touching.

"We don't have a mage," I sobbed as the baby continued to kick me.

"Yes, you do," Nico said, and dropped to his knees next to me. It was a tight fit, but they all made room.

"Nico," I sobbed, my ribs feeling like they were going to break more.

"Son, you need to stop hurting your mother," Nico said to my stomach.

The baby kicked again.

"Do it," Nico said.

I wasn't sure what he meant, but all of the guys touching my stomach, gripped my stomach a bit, and magic flowed from them into my stomach, and then into the baby.

But, the baby didn't stop.

"Siren," I gasped.

"No," Sharla whispered, her eyes wide.

The baby moved down, spun, and then kicked my other ribs, cracking one of them.

I closed my eyes, the pain almost unbearable as contractions began to come in rapid succession.

Another hand touched my stomach, and a new magic seeped in, instantly calming the baby.

I opened my eyes and Dad smiled at me. "Hello, Daughter."

"Dad," I sobbed.

"You didn't think I would miss my grandson being born, did you?" he asked and wiped the tears from my eyes.

"He keeps hurting her," Nico explained.

"I've got it," Dad said. He bent forward, and began singing Mom's lullaby.

The baby moved down again, his body going into the right position for birthing.

"Alright, hun. Push," Sharla ordered me, flipping the blanket up so she could see, but the others couldn't.

I pushed, and clutched Nico's hand with one of mine.

"You're doing great, love," he whispered.

"Again," Sharla said and smiled. "You're doing great."

I pushed, my body shuddering at the strain.

"I don't mean to hurry you," Nico whispered, "but the others need your magic."

I pushed again and again. And after another push, the baby slid out into Sharla's waiting arms.

Silver rushed over, cleaning out his nose and mouth, and the baby wailed.

I smiled and Nico kissed my lips softly. "You did great, Jolie."

Everyone moved back from me, no longer needing to touch my stomach.

Sharla pushed on my stomach and I gasped in pain.

"What are you doing?" I demanded.

"I've got to get the placenta out, hun. I'm sorry. I know it hurts, but I've got to do it," she said.

Fox ran to the door and his eyes widened when he saw his son. He looked up and our eyes met. "Are you okay?"

I nodded.

Sharla pushed again, and Fox's face drained of color as he saw what she was doing.

"Done," she announced.

Nico helped Silver clean up the baby, and then Dad cut the umbilical cord.

Everyone found a place away from me, averting their eyes, and Sharla pulled my top down.

Once he was ready, Nico set the baby on my naked chest.

"What's his name?" Nico asked me.

"Caleb," I whispered, cradling him close. "His name is Caleb."

"Hello, Caleb," Nico said.

Fox sat on my other side, smiling with tears in his eyes. "Hello, Caleb. Welcome to the family."

I cradled the adorable baby who had features from each of my mates, but most notably had Rhys's bright blue eyes.

Sharla cringed. "I need to stitch you up. Just a couple and then your mates' powers will heal you the rest of the way."

I nodded and then looked at the TV. There were thousands of beings fighting, the city was burning, and I couldn't tell who was winning.

"Fox, hold Caleb, please," I requested.

Fox took him, cradling him against his bare chest.

When had he taken his shirt off?

I pulled my shirt up, closed my eyes, and tapped each of my mate bonds. They tapped them back.

I looked at the screen, seeing Deryn overrun with goblins and dhampirs, Rhys battling demons, and the kings up to their necks in enemies. They didn't look like they were winning.

It was time.

I closed my eyes again, and gathered as much rage as I could. I opened my connections with them, and sent all of the rage I could to Rhys, Deryn, Emrys, Katar, and Dan.

I opened my eyes, watching as the five of them roared at the same time, and began flinging enemies like ragdolls.

"Damn," Nico whispered.

"Look, your daddies are killing lots of bad guys," Fox whispered to Caleb, who was curled up on his chest with his eyes closed.

They were killing a lot of people, but it wasn't enough.

"Crystals," I ordered Ezio.

Ezio ran out, then returned with dozens of crystals holding a ton of magic. They had been storing energy for me, and now was the time for me to use it. I grabbed a handful, sucked the energy into myself. Once I'd absorbed it, I focused on the bonds with the werewolves, and poured the rage down the pack bonds. Then, I focused on the dragons, and sent more.

"What's going on outside?" Nico asked Fox.

Fox gasped. "Shit, I forgot we were being attacked."

"I'll check," Ezio said and left.

"Jolie, don't overextend yourself," Nico ordered me.

I could hear the dragons and werewolves roaring on the TV.

"Crystals," I asked softly, my body so weak and tired.

He put more in my hands, and I drew it all in.

"Jolie, what are you doing?" Nico demanded.

I used my final two bonds, and sent all of the rage I could to the mages and elves.

"Holy shit," Dad whispered.

I opened my eyes, holding the rage, and drawing magic from the crystals to keep the rage going.

The tides had turned, and we were defeating the enemies.

I heard Andras roar outside, and hoped he was okay.

"We'll go assist," Declan said.

Everyone, but Nico, Dad, Sharla, the girls, and Silver left the bathroom.

"Jolie," Nico growled. "That's enough. You've helped enough."

"Just a bit longer," I gasped, taking the last crystals in my hands.

"You're going to kill yourself," Dad snapped. "Let it go!"

He was right. I was at my limit.

I released the power, but instead of drawing the rage back, I left it with the others. They would burn it out on their own.

I gasped and let my head drop as I released the crystals from my grip.

"Jolie?" Nico asked.

"I'm good," I panted.

"They're still enraged," Sharla said and looked at me.

I nodded. "I left the rage with them to burn off."

"You know how to do that?" she asked.

I shrugged and smirked. "Apparently."

"You are way more powerful than we thought," Dad said, pride coloring his tone.

"You need to try to feed him," Sharla said, taking Caleb from Nico and handing him to me.

"I'm going to go help outside," Dad said.

"I'm sorry I wasn't there earlier," Nico said, his eyes on his hands in his lap.

"Where were you?" I asked.

He sighed. "I've been tailing Trident Douche and Justina."

My eyes widened. "What?" I gasped. "For how long?"

He cringed. "Three or so months."

"You knew where they were for that long?" I asked, unsure whether to be angry or not.

"Yes, but I didn't want to tip them off or risk them attacking early," he explained. "Turned out it didn't matter."

"No, it didn't," Justina said from the doorway.

Nico stood up, putting a shield around the six of us still in the bathroom.

How had she gotten in?

Sharla backed up until she stood in front of her girls, crouched and ready to fight.

I couldn't sit up or stand yet, but I clutched Caleb to me. "Get out of here," I snarled.

"Oh, you've got a baby? Who is the lucky father?" she asked, snarling. "Doesn't matter. Once I'm done, none of you will be alive."

"You're not touching my mate or my child," Nico snarled, his staff in his hand.

She drew the knife she'd cut our bonds with and smiled at the fear she must have seen on my face. "I see you remember this blade. I'm going to enjoy severing your mate bonds with it."

If she severed our mate bonds, we'd be unable to form any new bonds. We would have no bonds left to make. No, I couldn't handle that. I couldn't let her sever the last bonds that we had.

Nico tapped his staff on the ground, and a blue circle spread around us. "You can't step foot in here," he told her.

She picked dirt out from under her nail with the dagger. "Oh, I don't need to get in there."

She threw the dagger, and Nico's smug smile of assurance that his shield would hold, disappeared as the dagger slipped right through, and embedded into his chest.

I screamed his name, and stood, holding Caleb in my arms as I went to Nico. He gasped in pain, blood pooling beneath him from the wound.

"No," I cried, and Caleb cried too.

Nico was dying. I could feel our bond fading. The bond flickered and dimmed slightly. Dammit! What could I do? I couldn't let him die, but I couldn't take the knife out. I couldn't heal him.

"Nico," I sobbed.

"You see, you just weren't meant to ever be happy. You're worthless and you're going to die, after I cut all of your bonds again, and kill everyone you love," Justina said, pulling another dagger from a sheath on her side.

I backed up until I stood just before Sharla, and handed her Caleb.

"Jolie," she whispered as she took him.

"Protect the children," I ordered her, my skin shifting into dragon's scales. I kissed Caleb's forehead, and he blinked at me. "I love you," I whispered into his bright blue eyes.

"You think you can win? How cute," Justina taunted.

I felt Deryn and Rhys tugging on our bonds, and I jerked them hard. I needed them and I needed them now.

"Any last words?" I asked her, shifted my hands into werewolf paws, and then gathered magic to me. I didn't have much, since I'd drained it all earlier, but I would use what I had.

"Jolie," Nico gasped.

"Help is coming," I assured Nico. "I'm going to take care of this once and for all."

"I'm going to enjoy hearing you cry when he dies," she said smugly.

"You are mine," I snarled at Justina.

Justina snarled back, and launched herself at me.

I slammed into her, sending her back into the hallway, and then stabbed her in the chest with my claws.

CHAPTER 26

JOLIE

Justina screamed, and I roared in her face, tossing her down the hallway.

Fox and Silver ran into the foyer, looking up at us on the second floor.

"Heal Nico!" I ordered them.

Fox snarled, unable to disobey my direct order. They both ran past me and into the bathroom.

"Got 'em trained finally, huh?" Justina asked, standing to her feet and wiping blood from her mouth.

"Stop talking, wench," I ordered her. I lunged forward, grabbed her by the throat, and tossed her out the nearest window. I leapt out of the window after her, landing in a crouch.

To my left, Ezio and the others were battling a large group of ogres and dhampirs. They glanced at me, eyes wide.

"Jolie!" Declan yelled.

"Defeat your enemies. I'm fine," I called back.

Justina stood and brushed herself off.

"Your death has been a long time coming," I told her. "I'm really going to fucking enjoy this."

She pulled out another dagger and flipped it in the air, smiling. "Let's dance, bitch."

She tried to cut my arm, but I had dragon scales covering it, which made the dagger just glance off. She snarled, furious.

Could I project my emotions to her? I'd done it with Trident Douche.

She continued to try to stab me, but I blocked with my arms, punched her a few times, and then kicked her in the stomach hard enough to send her sliding back on the grass.

"Fear," I whispered, thinking of being locked in the cupboard.

Her body trembled and her mouth popped open.

"That is what I felt when my father tortured me as a child," I told her. "He wasn't a good person. He was a murderer. A torturer. He deserved to die."

"You didn't know him," she snapped.

"No!" I snapped back. "You didn't know him. He blinded you with promises so you didn't see what a monster he truly was. We were friends! I would have never betrayed you. I would have saved you, but you let him use me. You were going to let him kill me! You're not a friend. You're pathetic."

"I'm pathetic? You're the one who latched onto the first guy who paid her any attention when she got here. Oh wait, make that *guys*. You're so terrified of being alone that you couldn't settle for one guy."

"*They* added me to their warrior's bond. I didn't add myself," I reminded her.

"Who wouldn't want a whore they could pass around?" she asked with a sneer.

I tried to punch her, but she dodged and sliced the blade across my cheek.

I screamed in pain, and stumbled back, my hand flying to the bleeding wound.

"You're nothing but trouble. All you do is bring chaos and destruction wherever you go. You should let me kill you, to save those boys from being brought down by you any further," she hissed.

"I am trouble," I agreed. "I was cursed. I brought that on them. But, I chose to remove the curse. I almost died removing that damn curse. So, they would be safe. I've trained for hours and hours, bleeding and bruised, so I could learn to protect myself. So I wouldn't be a burden. They love me, and I love them."

I couldn't hold the dragon scales on all of my body, so I just kept them in the vital parts like my throat and abdomen.

"Do they love you? Or did you use your siren powers to make them think they love you?"

"I don't have that ability," I told her.

"Just because mommy dearest from the beyond told you that, doesn't make it true," she snarled.

I gaped at her. "How did you know about that?"

She threw one of her daggers, and I barely managed to move so it didn't strike my heart. It did slice open my shoulder as it sailed over my arm, though.

I gasped in pain and growled.

"I can't believe Brayden was going to mate with you. Look at you! What do you have that these males keep falling for?" she screeched.

"Maybe it's because I'm not a fucking psycho like you!" I yelled, swinging at her.

She and I danced around each other, landing a few punches, but nothing significant.

I had to hurry and finish this or I would run out of energy. I was already dangerously low. I couldn't let her win. I had to kill her and get back to Caleb. I'd been away from him for too long as it was.

I stopped chasing her, centered myself, and opened my bond

with Rhys. He was close, but not close enough. I drew on his bond, letting my center grow warm.

She charged forward, and I opened my mouth, letting out a stream of flames.

She screamed and fell backwards, her hands covering her now burned face.

"Didn't know I could do that, did you?" I asked her smugly. I kicked the daggers out of her hands, and knelt by her. "No one fucking hurts my family. Had you killed me, this wouldn't have happened. If you hadn't cut my bonds, I would have left you alone. But, you destroyed me that day. You caused pain in my mates, a pain that haunts them to this day. That is something I cannot forgive."

"Fuck. You." she gasped.

"No, thanks. You're not my type," I replied.

Rhys and Deryn landed and helped attack the others, but when they looked over at me, they roared and headed towards us.

"Goodbye, Justina," I whispered. I picked up one of her daggers and stabbed her in the chest.

"That's rather inconvenient," Brayden said on a sigh behind me.

I spun, eyes wide, but it was too late. He grabbed my face, and darkness crowded my vision.

"No. Not this one, brother," Klaus said and knocked Brayden away from me.

I fell to my knees, gasping, as my vision returned to normal.

"What are you doing?" Brayden demanded. "You don't pick sides!"

"I pick her. You won't kill her or her child," Klaus said.

"Why are you protecting her?" Brayden snarled.

"Because she makes Nico happy," Klaus said. "And Nico deserves to be happy."

"What about me? Don't I deserve to be happy? She ruined my life!" Brayden snapped.

Deryn picked me up and moved away from the two brothers. "Baby, what are you doing out here?"

"How's Nico?" I asked instead of answering him.

"He's alive," Rhys said. "You would have felt it if he died."

He was right. I just wasn't thinking properly at the moment. Now that I wasn't fighting Justina, I was so tired.

"If you aren't with me, then you are against me," Brayden said.

"Don't do this," Klaus begged. "Please, don't make me fight you."

"Step out of the way, then," Brayden snapped, his bloodshot eyes deranged.

Klaus snapped his fingers and a staff, much like Nico's, appeared in his hand. "The line has been drawn. If you try to harm her or hers, I will defend them," Klaus said softly, calmly.

Brayden opened his mouth and started singing. I went to plug Deryn's ears, since he was holding me and couldn't do it himself, but he already had in the earplugs from Leona.

Klaus sighed, tapped his staff on the ground, and a bubble formed around the entire grounds of the house. He tapped again and a bubble formed around Brayden, locking his sound in with him. He flicked his finger, and Brayden, and the bubble he was in, moved out of the circle that encircled our grounds.

Klaus looked at me and smiled. "I'll take care of him, sister."

"Nico was stabbed," I told him.

His eyes widened and he glared down at Justina. "They planned this. Fine, I'm done playing pacifist."

"What are—" I didn't get to finish my question.

His eyes began to glow, the bubbles disappeared, and before Brayden could draw in a breath, Klaus clapped his hands together, and Brayden burst into a pile of ashes.

Deryn's and my mouths dropped open at the same time. I dropped my hands from Deryn's shoulders to stare at the ash pile.

Holy shit! That was some serious magic power.

I stared at the pile mutely.

"Is he really dead?" Deryn asked Klaus.

Klaus stopped glowing, and sighed, looking worn. "Yes."

Fox, Nico, and Silver came out of the house. Silver and Fox were holding Nico up between them.

"What are you doing?" I demanded.

"Why?" Nico asked Klaus instead of answering me.

Klaus smiled. "Your mate is doing good things for the world. Your baby will do even greater things." He looked at the pile that used to be Brayden. "And he was too far gone to be saved."

"He killed Dad," Nico said.

Klaus nodded, his lips pinched in a tight line. "I know."

Deryn walked to Nico, and let me hug him.

"How are you?" I asked him.

"Healing," he said. "How are you?"

"Tired," I admitted. I looked around. "Where's Rhys?"

Deryn turned so I could see where the last dhampirs were being killed by our troop.

"I need to see Caleb," I whispered.

"Caleb?" Deryn asked.

"Our son," I replied, smiling.

He smiled back. "I like that name. Caleb." He carried me upstairs, running when he heard Caleb crying, and Sharla immediately handed Caleb over when we entered the bathroom.

"Go feed him," she ordered me.

I bounced the crying infant in my arms, and Deryn carried us to the bedroom. I lay on my side, and began nursing him.

"He's beautiful," Deryn whispered as he stroked Caleb's dark hair, hair just like his.

"He is," I agreed.

"Dad's coming," he told me.

"My dad is here," I said.

"I saw him fighting outside."

"Can you get me some water?" I asked.

"I got it," Fox said, walked in the room, and handed me a cup with a straw.

I took a few small drinks and then handed the cup back to him.

"How's our boy doing?" Rhys asked, entering the room.

Caleb finished nursing, so I held him out to Rhys.

Rhys pulled his shirt off, and then took Caleb, cradling him against his chest, and making adorable noises to him.

I closed my eyes, resting now that it was over. It was finally over.

Tears slipped down my face, and Deryn climbed onto the bed behind me, wrapping his arms around me.

"It's over, baby. It's all over," he whispered.

Fox stroked my hair, sitting behind Deryn on the bed.

Rhys lay down beside me, putting Caleb between us.

Nico walked into the room, tugged Rhys off the bed, and took his place. He set his hand on my cheek. "Don't you ever do that again."

"You were dying," I whispered.

"I would never leave you, darling." He smiled and kissed my lips lightly. He looked down at our sleeping son and smiled. "He's got Rhys's eyes."

"Your nose," Rhys said to Nico.

"My hair," Deryn said.

"My jaw," Fox said.

"He's perfect," I sniffled.

Deryn kissed my shoulder, and I realized that I was naked.

"Why didn't you tell me I was naked?" I asked.

"We thought you knew," Rhys said with a chuckle.

"Are you telling me that I fought Justina while naked? And that Klaus and Brayden saw me naked?"

"Yeah," Nico said and chuckled. "As did everyone else who was fighting outside."

I threw my head back and laughed, then clutched at my stomach and grunted in pain.

"You need to lay here and rest," Nico ordered me.

"So, do you," Rhys said. "You're not completely healed either."

Caleb started to fuss, and then we all stared in disbelief as he turned into a wolf pup.

"That is not normal," Deryn informed us.

"I need clothes," I said. "The kings are going to want to see him, and I don't want to be naked in front of my fathers." Well, apparently, I'd already been naked outside, which my dad had seen. Whoops.

Rhys grabbed sweatpants from the dresser, and helped me put them on while still laying down. He then helped me put a nursing tank top on that had convenient snaps to let me pull out a boob to feed Caleb without pulling up my entire shirt.

"Now, rest. We'll feed everyone, and that should give you enough time to fully recover," Rhys said. He looked at the wolf pup now in our bed and smiled. "He's adorable."

I snuggled closer to Caleb, wrapping myself around him like a human cocoon.

"Yes, he is," I whispered happily, a huge smile on my face as I closed my eyes.

Nico lay behind me, put one arm beneath my pillow, and one around my stomach.

I was just about to fall asleep, when Sharla came in and pushed on my stomach several times, which hurt.

"Ouch," I growled at her without opening my eyes.

"Shush. We have to do this to ensure your uterus tightens up correctly. Go back to sleep," she ordered me, and then left.

Caleb shifted back into human form, so I tugged a blanket up to just below his belly button, wrapped my arm around his side, and cuddled him against the top of my chest, which was bare, so our skin was in contact. He sniffed loudly a few times then settled and went to sleep.

CHAPTER 27

FOXFIRE

"She gave me an order," I whispered to Rhys as we stood outside the bedroom, watching her, Nico, and Caleb sleep.

"What?" he asked. "When?"

"I came in when Justina was fighting her. I was going to kill that wench, but Jolie ordered me to heal Nico. She didn't ask. She ordered me to do it. Then she tossed Justina out the window."

"Wow," Rhys whispered.

I nodded. "It was so hot watching her throw the bitch out the window," I admitted.

He chuckled. "I'm still surprised she gave you an order. She usually tries to avoid doing that."

I nodded again. "I was really surprised. I was also pissed because I wanted to kill Justina, but it was clear she wanted to do it. I don't know how the heck she had the energy to do it. She'd just given birth, used all of the crystals to send out the rage power to everyone, and then she fought Justina."

"Wait, she used *all* of the crystals?" Rhys asked, eyes wide as he turned to face me fully.

I gently shut the door, and led him away from the room. Those three needed some rest. Soon, our parents would be here and demanding to see them.

"Yes. She used all of them. She grabbed fistfuls of them."

"I didn't even know she could send it to everyone," Rhys whispered. "I couldn't believe my eyes when even the weakest dragons of our clan were taking warrior forms."

"If we hadn't invited her exes here, I don't know if she would have survived delivery. Caleb was fighting her and Sharla said she had started to panic until they showed up," I told him.

"I'm glad Silver thought to let us know of the possibility," Rhys whispered.

"Yeah, I'm going to have to buy him an extra present this year," I said and then chuckled.

"My scales seem to be working again," Rhys said. "Not sure what fixed it, but I'm back to normal."

"Maybe you just needed a child to motivate you to become stronger," I said with a smirk.

Rhys shrugged. "Whatever it was, I'm glad."

The front door flew open, and we both raced to the stairs, stepping into Dan's path.

"Wait," I ordered him.

He glared down at me. "Where is she?"

"She's sleeping. She battled Justina after giving birth and sending us that power. She needs to sleep for at least an hour. We'll get you and the others some food, and then you can meet your grandson," I explained.

He glared at me, but then gave a slight nod, and stomped down to the dining room.

I exhaled. "He still scares me."

"Only a fool wouldn't be scared of Dan," Rhys whispered.

"He almost broke my jaw while we were sparring when Jolie

enraged him," I muttered and rubbed at the phantom pain in my jaw.

Rhys clapped me on the shoulder and smiled. "Better you than me."

"You're such a good friend," I teased.

His parents entered, and he escorted them to the dining room.

I waited by the door for my parents, knowing they'd want to rush upstairs.

The entered, ignored me, and started to head up the stairs.

"Hey," I snapped at them.

They turned.

"She's sleeping," I said. "Leave her be for a bit."

"I'm going to heal her," Mother said. "Katar, go with your son."

"Mom," I sighed.

Dad draped his arm around my shoulders and tugged me away. "Come on, let's go get food ready. Your mate is going to be ravenous when she wakes up."

"Isn't that how she is whenever she wakes up?" I asked with a smirk.

Dad laughed. "Too true."

"So, any casualties?" I asked when we entered the room where Emrys, Adelaide, Declan, Rhys, Dan, Kylan, Ezio, Deryn, Silver, Dalton, Klaus, Martin, Sharla, Madison, Tamara and Yukio sat around our table.

Everyone shook their heads.

Wow. Jolie had no idea what she'd accomplished by enraging everyone. Normally, there were at least a dozen casualties in a battle that large.

"What are we eating?" Dad asked.

"Pizza," Rhys announced.

"It was the easiest and fastest thing we could get," Deryn explained.

"Are there any shops open?" I asked, thinking of the destruction I had seen going on in the city.

"Our shop is always open," Dan said with a wide smile.

I sat down, and leaned my head on my arms on the table. I was so tired.

"So, what is our grandson's name?" Dan asked.

"No," Deryn said immediately. "Jolie can introduce him when he comes down."

"Did you tell him?" Rhys asked Deryn.

"Tell me what?" Dan asked.

Deryn shook his head, smirking. "I want to see his reaction when it happens."

Dan scowled. "If there's something wrong—"

"It's not wrong," Deryn said and then scowled. "I don't think."

"That's super reassuring, Son," Dan grumbled.

Mom returned, kissed the back of my head, and sat beside me. "She's still sleeping," she advised everyone. "But, she's healthy and so is the baby and Nico."

"He almost died," I whispered, remembering that awful pain in my chest when the knife had gone into his.

"Where's that dagger?" Emrys asked.

"I put it in our vault," Rhys answered. "I'll give it to you three to decide what you want to do with it."

"We should just give it to the elders," I suggested.

Dan nodded. "That's my vote, too."

What? Dan agreed with me on something for once?

"I agree," Dad said.

Thor and Leona entered, and Leona searched the room, her eyes wide and frantic.

"Where is she?" she demanded.

"She's sleeping," Kara told her.

"Is she—"

"She's fine," Dalton assured her.

"But, all that power," Leona whispered.

Dalton nodded. "I know. It surprised me, too. She used dozens of crystals with stored magical energy to pull it off, but she is fine. Kara just went and checked on her."

Leona sagged into Thor, who wrapped his arm around her waist to hold her against his side.

"See, I told you she was fine," Thor whispered. "Jolie is resilient."

"Like a cockroach," Adelaide said.

Several around the room growled, myself included.

She scoffed and rolled her eyes. "I didn't mean it as an insult. Just that things which should normally kill one of her kind, she lives through. It's quite remarkable."

"Says the villain as she debates dissecting her," I whispered to Dad.

Dad snorted as he tried to keep his laughter in, and Mother pinched my side.

"Let's make the table bigger," I said to Rhys.

Everyone stood, and backed up a few steps. Rhys and I hit the buttons on each side of the table, then shoved it apart at the seam. The table was magical, and could seat anywhere from four to thirty. I was glad Rhys had designed the room to be so large. The first time I'd entered, I had thought it was ridiculously over-sized, but now I understood his reasoning.

Mother set her hand on the back of my head, and I felt her warm energy filling me.

"Mom," I mumbled.

"Hush. You're tired and your mate needs you at one hundred percent, so she doesn't have to be the only one dealing with the baby," she told me.

I wouldn't argue with her on that. Plus, I felt like I had failed Jolie today. She'd been injured fighting Justina, when we had all agreed not to let her fight her. If she hadn't ordered me away, I would have killed Justina immediately.

"Why are you scowling?" Dad asked.

"Nothing," I lied.

He arched a brow at me.

I waved my hand. "It's really nothing. I'm just brooding."

The doorbell rang, and we all cringed when we heard Caleb cry.

"Whoops," Rhys said as he stood. "I hadn't thought about the doorbell waking him."

"You may want to unhook it until he's a bit older," Adelaide suggested.

I stood as well, knowing he would need help carrying the boxes.

The werewolf at the door looked stressed, but smiled as he spoke to us, and made three trips for all of the pizzas they had ordered.

We set them out on the table, then passed around paper plates.

"Here, you all are," Jolie said as she entered the room.

Deryn, Rhys, and I rushed to her side.

Caleb's eyes were closed again, and he was in human form. I looked at his ears and felt a smile tug up my lips. His ears were pointed at the top, something I had missed before.

"Stop hogging them," Adelaide complained.

Jolie stepped away from us, turned Caleb so he was leaning back against her chest, facing everyone in the room, with her arm around him and one under his butt. "Everyone, this is Caleb."

All of the grandparents started to stand, but then all froze.

"Dalton, you go," Dan said. "We've had chances to bond with him while he was in her womb."

Dalton smiled appreciatively, then walked to Jolie. He kissed her forehead and her eyes closed a moment as her smile spread. Dalton rested his forehead against Caleb's and whispered to him.

Caleb opened his eyes and made a cooing sound.

Dalton stepped back and turned his head away as he tried to discreetly wipe his eyes.

"My turn!" Dan said and rushed over. He kissed Jolie's cheek. "How are you feeling?"

"Tired, but good," she said.

Dan looked down at Caleb, bending so he was eye level with the child. "Hello, Son."

Caleb met Dan's eyes, then shifted into a wolf pup in Jolie's arms.

Dan's eyes widened and his mouth dropped open.

"That was the secret I was keeping," Deryn said, chuckling. "And it was so worth it to see your face."

"That's not normal?" Dalton asked.

Dan shook his head. "They're usually not able to shift until around five years old."

"He shifted in vitro," Kara told him.

"We thought we'd all hallucinated it," Deryn said. "Clearly, we hadn't."

"That's remarkable," Dan said. He brushed his fingers across Caleb's head, between his ears. "You're perfect, little one."

"Caleb," Jolie reminded him.

Dan smirked. "Yes, Caleb."

Caleb shifted back, and Jolie shifted her hold on him, so he lay on her arm, with his butt against the bend in her elbow, and his head in her palm. He seemed to enjoy that position.

"Who's next?" she asked, looking up with a wide smile.

Perfect. Yes. Those two were perfect.

I looked at my brothers, and saw the same feeling reflected in their eyes.

CHAPTER 28

JOLIE

"Caleb, don't bite so hard," I growled at the rambunctious six-month-old.

Caleb opened his jaws, his needle-sharp puppy teeth loosening from my finger.

"Thank you," I whispered and ruffled his ears.

Deryn bounded up to us in his wolf form, wagging his tail with his tongue lolling out the side of his mouth.

Caleb yipped in delight, and ran to Deryn, rubbing along his legs, looking more like a cat than a wolf.

"Your turn," I told Deryn, and headed towards the house.

I cast one glance back, watching as the father and son ran into the forest to play.

"Ready?" Fox asked.

I yelped, since I hadn't heard him approach. "What?" I asked.

He smiled and then bowed. "Would you accompany me, my queen?"

I smiled back. "Okay."

He wrapped his arms around me, spun around, and dipped

me as he kissed me. My head spun, and I wrapped my arms around his neck, even though I knew he would never drop me.

"Where are we going?" I asked when he righted us.

"Come on and you'll find out," he said, slipping his fingers between mine, and tugging me along.

I chuckled at my kind-hearted mate, and jogged along behind him. He led me to one of Dan's SUVs, where Ezio stood, waiting for us.

"Ready?" Ezio asked.

Fox nodded, and ushered me into the back seat.

Once we were buckled, Ezio drove out, whispering conspiratorially to Fox.

"What's going on?" I asked.

"You'll see," Fox said. "I'm not going to ruin it."

We pulled into a car dealership, and I looked at Fox, but he wasn't looking at me. When we stopped, Fox leapt out, and opened the door for me.

"Come on," he hurried me, took my hand, and led me to the middle of the lot, where Rhys stood with a car salesman.

Rhys kissed my cheek, and spread his arms. "Pick one."

I blinked. "What?"

"You don't have a car," Rhys said.

"And, we think it is time that you have one of your own," Fox added.

"You mean...I won't have a driver or bodyguard assigned to me?" I asked, my mouth open in disbelief.

Rhys picked up one of my hands and said, "We would prefer you to have a driver, ten bodyguards, and a dozen more on backup, but we know that you can take care of yourself. You proved that when you gave birth to a child, used your power to save the city, and then defeated Justina. We are overprotective jerks at times, and we are trying to work on that."

"So, we are taking this first step, by giving you a car of your own. One that you can drive wherever you want to go. We would still prefer if you took someone with you, but it's not something we are going to require. We want you to be safe, but we want you to be happy first and foremost," Fox said.

I hugged them both, and then looked at the cars around me. There was every type of car, and I didn't know where to start. So, I just walked to each car I liked, and inspected it. I narrowed it down to two cars, test drove them, and then picked the winner. A cute sports car that had enough room for four people, or three people and a baby car seat. I got it in white.

"Dan's going to have some improvements done to it, so you'll get it in about a week," Rhys told me.

I snickered. "Of course, Dan is."

"Let's go get the paperwork finalized," the salesman said.

I walked between Rhys and Fox, holding each of their hands.

"Thank you," I said, smiling up at them. "This really means a lot to me."

They each squeezed my hand, smiling in response.

I expected us to go to our house, but instead, they drove to Dan's pizza restaurant. When we walked in, my eyes widened at the huge crowd gathered. Emrys, Adelaide, Katar, Kara, Silverowl, Andras, Gavin, Gavin's human girlfriend, Mawrth, Rhian, Brenin, Dan, Deryn, Caleb, Ezio, Yukio, Declan, Martin, Sharla, Tamara, Madison, Zelphar, Kylan, Tobias, Lorenzo, Thor, Leona, Nico, and Tawny were all there.

"What's going on?" I asked.

"Happy birthday!" everyone yelled.

My mouth gaped open and shut, like a fish out of water. It was my birthday? I had totally forgotten!

The front door opened, and Dad, Colton, and Sam walked in, carrying a huge cake. They started singing, and the rest of them joined in.

Tears brimmed, as all of the people I cared about the most sang to me. I blew out the candles, but didn't have a single thing to wish for. I had everything I ever wanted or needed, right here.

Thanks for reading!

www.CatherineBanks.com

Newsletter
http://catbanks.co/newsletter

ABOUT THE AUTHOR

Catherine Banks is a USA Today bestselling fantasy author who writes in several fantasy subgenres under two pseudonyms. She began writing fiction at only four years old and finished her first full-length novel at the age of fifteen. She is married to her soulmate and best friend, Avery, who she has two amazing children with. After her full-time job, she reads books, plays video games, and watches anime shows and movies with her family to relax. Although she has lived in Northern California her entire life, she dreams of traveling around the world. Catherine is also C.E.O. of Turbo Kitten Industries™, a company with many hats including being a book publisher and Etsy store full of nerdy fun.

CONNECT WITH CATHERINE BANKS

I really appreciate you reading my book! Here are some ways to connect with me:
www.catherinebanks.com

Follow me on BookBub:
https://www.bookbub.com/authors/catherine-banks

Join my newsletter for deals and snippets:
http://Catbanks.co/newsletter

Like my author Facebook page:
http://www.Facebook.com/CatherineBanksAuthor

Follow me on Twitter:
http://www.Twitter.com/catherineebanks

Follow me on Goodreads:
http://www.Goodreads.com/catherine_banks

www.Turbokitten.us
www.Turbokitten.us/catherine-banks

Purchase items handmade by Catherine:
http://Etsy.com/shop/TurboKittenInd

Alys of Asgard
Tiger Tears
Calvin's Alien Adventure
Sybil Deceived
Olansia
Lion About
The Pawn